She was touching Cade because she wanted to.

The simple purity and comfort of a human connection, a touch that didn't involve menace or pain.

Yes, it had to be that, she told herself.

The hand was warm as it cupped the flare of her hip bone. When the hand slid across her belly and curved to her waist where she lay on her side in the bed of the pickup, she didn't resist an automatic movement to relax into the heat of his body, curled behind her.

In the humidity, it was only moments before she felt the hollow of her spine grow damp with perspiration, but still the heat was welcome. To be close to another body, without fear, without trembling...it was both all she had wished and more than she had dared to hope for in the past year.

His hand slid, as if in sleep, gently along her rib cage. Abby wondered if he could feel the sudden slamming acceleration of her heartbeat, or the manic trembling that was turning her insides to liquid.

Mel Sterling started writing stories in elementary school and wrote her first full-length novel in a spiral-bound notebook at age twelve. Her favorite Christmas present was a typewriter and a ream of paper. After college, she found herself programming computers and writing technical documentation. A few years ago, she rediscovered romance writing during a prolonged period of insomnia and began to indulge her passion with a vengeance. She lives with her computer geek husband in a quiet, happy house full of books, animals and ideas.

DANGEROUS ESCAPE

MEL STERLING

Previously published as *Latimer's Law*

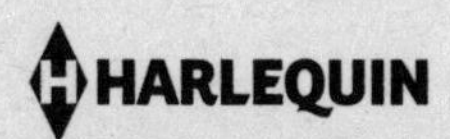

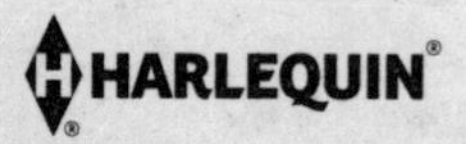

Recycling programs for this product may not exist in your area.

ISBN-13: 978-1-335-74491-3

Dangerous Escape

First published as Latimer's Law in 2014.
This edition published in 2022.

For questions and comments about the quality of this book, please contact us at CustomerService@Harlequin.com.

Harlequin Enterprises ULC
22 Adelaide St. West, 41st Floor
Toronto, Ontario M5H 4E3, Canada
www.Harlequin.com

Printed in U.S.A.

DANGEROUS ESCAPE

For my husband, the best and most honorable man I know. Thank you for giving me the freedom to run.

Chapter 1

The last straw was a single, ridiculous button.

Abby shifted the paper grocery sack in her arms as she stepped out of the convenience store. The hard plastic cap of the orange juice nudged at just the wrong place, the curve under her biceps where the bruises had never quite faded in the past few months. No bruises where they couldn't be covered. Long practice brought skill. She moved the sack again, and a button burst from her worn chambray shirt.

She followed the button's freewheeling path across the concrete sidewalk until it plummeted off the curb. It bounced across the white stripe of a parking space and into the black shadow beneath a pickup truck. With a sigh, Abby went around the half-open driver's door, looking apologetically into the cab. How to explain she needed the driver to move the truck so she could find a button? She couldn't come home from the store with that particular button missing, right at the shadowed hollow between her breasts—well. It was unthinkable. Her mind raced ahead, picturing the scenario. She could drop the button on the floor when she put the sack on the kitchen counter, as if it had come loose at that very moment. The trick could work, but only if she had the button.

The pickup was empty.

Empty.

With the keys in the ignition, and the engine running.

The shimmering brilliance of an impossible, desperate solution forced all the air out of Abby's lungs.

Escape.

Abby didn't glance toward the store or look around for the truck's driver. She dumped the grocery bag into the passenger seat and hoisted herself in behind the wheel, feeling the soreness in her arms and back. She yanked the door closed and settled into the seat.

Three pedals on the floor, gearshift in neutral on the column, parking brake set.

Her heart lurched. She couldn't let herself think

beyond the physical mechanics of making the truck go. She stretched her leg to stomp the clutch, studied the gearshift a moment and worked it into reverse. Maybe six years since she'd driven a manual transmission, and months since she'd driven at all. The bank repossessed the car when she couldn't make the payments, but before that there'd been a series of repairs that consumed the meager savings she and her husband, Gary, had scraped together. What didn't go into the adult day care business went to the mechanic.

Fate was kind. Abby managed not to stall as the truck groaned into reverse out of the parking space. She rode the crow-hopping lurches into first gear, pulling herself close to the steering wheel because the seat was too far back, but there was no time to adjust it. Something heavy fell over in the covered bed of the truck and Abby felt a gut-punch of guilt.

She was stealing a truck.

This wasn't in the same league as keeping the change she found in the washing machine or behind sofa cushions, or filching a five from the grocery money when she thought Marsh wouldn't notice. This was a felony. *Grand theft, auto,* her rap sheet would read.

Was she out of her mind?

How fast could she get out of sight? It wouldn't

be long before the truck's owner called the police—minutes, maybe.

How bad could jail be, in comparison with her life?

Left turn from the parking lot. Left again at the four-way stop, hands jittering on the wheel, stomach churning. Then straight on to the interstate, heading north, grinding gears as her speed increased.

A few miles past the town line, still hunched over the steering wheel, Abby realized the roar she was hearing was the truck's engine under strain. She was pushing ninety, screaming to be noticed by the highway patrol, followed by a ticket if she were very lucky, more likely arrested when she couldn't produce insurance and registration. She stood out like a white gull on blacktop, in the red truck on the mostly empty road. She had to calm down, think about what came next.

She rolled down the window to catch the breeze, too stressed to decipher the air-conditioning controls. The Florida summer heat was making her dizzy. She needed to get her heart rate down. Try to still the shaking in her hands and stop jerking the truck all over the lane, another attention-getter she couldn't afford.

First things first. Get off the interstate, travel the secondary roads. Keep moving. Head for Gainesville, maybe, a bigger town than Wildwood, where she could ditch the truck and use public transportation. She wondered if there was a map in the glove box. She was so overwhelmed by what she'd done that she couldn't remember the names of towns in the county where she'd lived more than half her life.

Money would be an issue immediately. She didn't dare use the credit card—it would give her away. In the hip pocket of her jeans there was only the envelope of fifty-odd dollars, whatever she'd managed to scrounge in the past fifteen months. She had the change from the two twenties Gary's brother, Marsh, had given her for the market. Whenever she left the house, she always carried her stash with her. She knew Marsh went through her room. Any day he might find the loose baseboard molding in the back of the closet where she had cut a small hole in the drywall and hidden her hoard.

Marsh.

How did he know she needed the anchor of his touch when he tucked her hand in his elbow? The reality of his wool suit jacket. The faint humidity Abby could sense there at the bend of his arm, with her fingers gently covered by his free hand. She'd thought she was done with tears, until the motorized hoist began to lower Gary's coffin into the earth. It seemed somehow sterile and impolite for a funeral to be such an automated and regulated event.

Marsh understood. She heard him draw a harsh breath as the casket's top slipped below ground level. His hand tightened on hers. How could they just put Gary into the earth? How could they cover him up with foot after foot of dirt? She couldn't breathe, thinking about it.

Thank God Marsh was here. She'd still be dithering uselessly about whether red or white satin should line the box where Gary would lie forever, never turning his too-hot pillow to the cooler side.

Marsh. Damn his rat-bastard-needed-to-be-shot hide.

And while she was at it, damn her own stupid hide for skidding down the slippery slope that had led to this moment, careening along the interstate in a stolen pickup, in the middle of the hottest summer she could remember, roasting in the long sleeves that covered the bruises. The only positive was that the tears, so quick to spring since Gary died, were nowhere to be found.

A green marker sign grew in the distance, and Abby recognized something at last: Micanopy, an even smaller, more backward town than Wildwood. She recalled a narrow road winding through pecan orchards, the occasional orange grove and state forestland. It would eventually lead to Gainesville. She eased her foot off the accelerator and signaled for the exit. Only a mile down the narrow road was an intersection with a numbered state forest road. She paused, checking for other cars, thinking hard. From a camping trip in the early days of her marriage to Gary, Abby recalled a campground several miles into the state forest. If nothing else, its location next to a tea-dark river would help calm her. Flowing water always did. She had to get control of herself before she did something even more stupid.

Abby downshifted and turned the truck off the paved road onto the graded gray marl of the forestry access. The tires raised clouds of silty dust in the heat, and she slowed even more to leave less of a trail, as if Marsh could see her from Wildwood. Best to get out of sight altogether while she took stock of her situation. And maybe, just maybe, leave the truck behind and make her way back to Micanopy. She could hitchhike into Gainesville. It wouldn't be safe, but at least she wouldn't be caught in a stolen truck.

The unpaved road was in poor condition. Summer downpours had rutted it from crown to edge, jouncing her, jarring her torso and tossing the heavy things in the bed of the truck around again. Twenty minutes later she located the loop drive of the tiny campground and circled it, glad to find the place completely empty. With a shuddering sigh of relief, Abby circled a second time and angle-parked the truck into the most secluded of the eight campsites to conceal its license plates. She turned off the engine. For a long moment she stared at the river flowing past thirty feet away, watching a water-darkened stick curl downstream. Then she put her head on the steering wheel and gave in to the shakes that had threatened to overtake her for the past hour and a half.

She, Abigail McMurray, former straight-A student and all-around good egg, had stolen a truck.

She'd run away from home, what little remained of it now that she'd given up so much to Marsh. A giant bubble of guilt welled and burst in her chest. Those poor people, the adults who came to the house for day care and respite for their own caregivers. Only Marsh was there now. She was horrified to think he might take out his ire on one of the sweet people who trusted her to shelter them, feed them healthy meals and make sure Rosemary didn't hog the DVD remote during Movie Hour.

She should turn around, *now,* and go back.

She *couldn't* turn around now and go back.

But she could. After dark she could go home, leave the truck in the drugstore parking lot a mile from the convenience store where she'd taken it and sneak away. After wiping down the interior to remove her fingerprints. She could leave a note of apology and money for gas. The police would find the truck soon enough. It could all go away. It would be as if it had never happened.

Except for Marsh's anger. His anger, and his fists.

Abby's stomach clenched. Her mouth was dry. She'd been gritting her teeth for miles and miles—a monstrous tension headache throbbed at her temples. Maybe some juice would help. She started to reach for the jug, but it only reminded her of the impetus for her flight.

She bit her lip and grabbed the jug anyway, wrenching it open with fierce determination, and downed several swallows of the juice. It was only orange juice, after all, not an enemy, not a symbol, not Marsh's grip. When she had capped the jug again, she got out of the truck to stretch her legs and face what she'd done head-on. Time to be practical about it all.... If she wasn't going to take the truck back, she might as well see if anything in the pickup bed could be of any use to her in her new life of crime.

The fork, covered with mayonnaise and bits of tuna, clattered into the sink with a noise that hurt her ears. Abby felt the familiar black wave of grief submerge her. It was all too much. Tuna. Peanut butter. Sandwiches. Tomato soup. Toast. Apple wedges. Cheese. Celery sticks. Wheelchairs. Adult diapers. Tantrums. Seizures. Without Gary, it was too much.

"What is it? What's wrong, Abigail?"

"I can't. I need Gary. I can't do this."

"You can. We *can. Look, I'm here. Just tell me...how many tuna sandwiches?"*

Abby slid down the cupboard doors by the sink

and sat on the floor with her knees drawn up and her head pressed against them. "I don't know."

Marsh put a warm hand on her shoulder. "Then tell me who gets peanut butter. I can manage that, I know. Come on, Abigail. It'll be all right. All we need is time." His voice was serene and placid. When he spoke, she could think again. Maybe it would work. Maybe all it took was time. Maybe he was right. He smelled like Gary. She wiped her eyes against the knees of her jeans.

"Rosemary. Rosemary gets peanut butter. Joe gets tuna."

"Good, good. The older guy, is his name Smith? What kind of sandwich does he get?"

The old red truck had a white camper shell over the bed of the pickup. Tinted windows prevented her from peering in, so she went to the back of the truck and turned the handle, lifting the hatch…

…and found herself staring into the unwavering barrel of a pistol, held beneath the grimmest, bluest gaze she'd ever seen, a blue gaze bracketed on one side by a starburst of corrugated scar tissue, and a smear of blood on the other. Standing at the shoulder of the man with the gun was a German shepherd, teeth bared and hackles raised.

When his pickup lurched into motion, Cade Latimer toppled from his crouch, striking his head on the big green toolbox. He had left the K-9 training facility outside Bushnell a few minutes ago and had pulled off the interstate at the Wildwood exit only to get a bad cup of convenience store coffee for the road and give Mort a snack and a drink of water. He'd climbed into the bed of the truck to tend to Mort before they got back on the road to head to the northeast corner of Alabama for some decent hill country hiking, fishing and camping.

His first reaction was to right himself and lunge for the back of the truck—he must have forgotten to set the parking brake, and the truck had slipped into reverse. He had a vision of his truck rolling slowly out of control and into the street, causing the sort of stupid accident he had always hated to see while on patrol duty in the sheriff's department. Before his undercover days, how many times had he lectured drivers about putting on their thinking caps before getting behind the wheel of a two-ton killing machine? But then he got a glimpse of someone in the cab of his pickup, behind the wheel, and realized something else was going on. Something illegal.

For a moment Cade couldn't believe it was happening. Surely no one in this Podunk, backwater, stuck-in-the-Depression town would steal a truck. Weren't small-town folk supposed to be as honest as the day was long? A second lurching hop sent him flat again. Mort scrabbled uselessly, claws squealing against metal as the truck fishtailed onto the road. Cade reached out to steady his dog and spoke the command for the German shepherd to lie down. Warm wetness trickled down from Cade's scalp. He'd cut himself on the metal toolbox.

One last bump, then the truck's motion smoothed and Cade ventured to look out the side window.

Interstate. Passing swiftly.

Damn it.

He peered through the darkly tinted camper shell window into the cab of the truck and wished—not for the first time—that he'd had the cab's window replaced with a slider. Most often he thought about that when he wanted to check on Mort while the truck was in motion, but now he wanted the slider so he could strangle the jerk who'd stolen his truck.

With Cade in it, no less.

Cade expected to see some punk-ass kid, maybe two, with cigarettes hanging loosely from their lips and leaving ash all over his vintage bench seat, out for a joyride with a six-pack of cheap beer. Instead, he saw the clean profile of a woman, light brown hair scraped back in a bobbing ponytail that brushed her back below her shoulder blades, and in the seat next to her wobbled a sack of groceries.

Groceries!

Some redneck soccer mom had stolen his truck. Maybe she was drunk already, though it wasn't even ten in the morning, and confused which truck in the parking lot was hers.

Blood dripped from his jaw onto his neck. Cade reached into his back pocket for a bandanna. Blotting, he looked at the cloth and saw the bright blossom of red there. Scalp wound. A tentative probe with his fingertips showed the cut was neither long nor deep, though it felt tender and was already swelling. The woman had caught him completely off guard. It shouldn't have happened. His personal radar should have been better. He was a K-9 deputy, for crying out loud. It was his job to pay attention. Just because he was on vacation was no reason to check his brain at the door.

What was worse, he knew not to leave his keys in and the engine running, even if it was only going to be for the two minutes he was feeding Mort. Talk about putting on his thinking cap.... He'd grown soft in the two years since he'd had to leave undercover work at the Marion County Sheriff's Department after his accident. It was disturbing to realize how much he'd come to depend on Mort's alertness to supplement his own training, awareness and common sense. Cade glared at the woman impotently, peering past her at the speedometer needle as it crept up and up. He watched her hands shaking on the steering wheel. She was all over the damned road. Drunk, high or terrified by what she'd done?

Staying low, not wanting her to glance in the rearview and see even a shadow of him crouching in the pickup's bed, Cade shifted toward the tailgate again, edging past his camping gear and fishing tackle, cooler, bedroll and tools. He leaned out cautiously, studied the concrete of the interstate flashing by at high speed beneath him and brought the flap of the truck's canopy down. He latched it securely to shut out the boil of the truck's slipstream, then glanced over his shoulder to see if she'd noticed. Her face was still turned toward the front, and she was scooted toward the wheel as if she hadn't bothered to pull the bench seat forward to accommodate her height.

Still at the back of the bed, Cade settled low and opened his zippered duffel. The 9mm Beretta waited there in its pocket holster, safety on, with a full clip and a bullet chambered. He stuck it in the back of his jeans, and slipped a couple of heavy-duty cable ties out of the same bag. He formed them into a two-link chain before settling low again, in case she pulled another thank-you-ma'am across the roadway. Not much he could do at the moment, but by God, when she stopped—he'd be ready.

She'd stolen the wrong truck.

Chapter 2

"Hands up, lady."

Abby's shocked gaze traveled slowly up from the menacing dark little mouth at the end of the gun barrel to the blue eyes behind it, and locked there. Peripheral vision showed her the shiny, puckered nightmare flesh of an old acid burn fanning out from the edge of his left eye toward his hairline and ear, and spilling down the side of his neck to vanish beneath his clothing. A vision of splattered melted red candle wax flashed through her mind. It took her too long to look away from the damaged skin, and the man's eyes narrowed in irritation at her visible shock and revulsion. When her gaze finally hitched away from the terrible visage, she barely noticed the rest of his appearance. He wore jeans and a T-shirt, and a khaki fishing vest full of pockets. Her hands rose slowly on their own, the truck keys dangling from her left. Her own terror and guilt made her babble.

"Oh, God. Oh, God. I'm sorry. It was a mistake. I didn't mean to—"

"Shut up. Turn around. Drop the keys. Down on your knees."

"You ought to be down on your knees to me, Abigail. It isn't every man who'll take on his brother's widow and his business and make it all work."

"I know. I know. It's just that...it's the checking account. It's the last thing with his name on it. It's so hard to let go."

"It's been six months. Gary's not walking through that door ever again."

"Stop it! Just...stop."

"Ah... I didn't mean to make you cry. I don't want to hurt you. Why do you make me say these things, Abby? Why?"

"I'm sorry. I know you don't mean to..."

"Come here. Dry your eyes. It won't look good at the bank when we change the names on the account if your face is puffy."

Abby stared. With one hand the man reached out to open the tailgate while the other held the gun pointed at her. "I said on your knees, woman!"

Some final anchoring cord of rationality

snapped inside Abby. "You can't speak to me like that!"

His unbelieving laugh was deep and rich as he slid off the tailgate and stood. "This, from the nut-job who stole my truck with me inside it? Mort, *fass.*" At the single command, the dog leaped out of the truck and put his nose against Abby's thigh, growling. "Turn around. On your knees. Do it now."

Abby's heart pounded. In her head she saw herself at dog-level, her bare throat torn and bloodied by the teeth of the menacing shepherd. Or her brains splattered on the sand of the campsite by a single shot from that beast of a gun. She turned slowly away from the tall, blue-eyed man, dropped the keys in the sand and went to her knees. The dog's nose shifted to her shoulder and the growling continued.

"Hands on your head."

She obeyed, lacing her fingers. "Please don't let him bite me." She could hear the trembling in her own voice. Fear spiked sharp and bitter in her mouth and she thought the orange juice might make a reappearance. She had the same feeling of horrible dread when Marsh was displeased.

"I'll tell you when you can talk." His foot nudged her ankles apart and then the sole of his work boot settled lightly on her calf.

The man grasped Abby's left forearm and

brought her hand behind her back, then joined the right to it with a grating ratchet. He had shackled her—not with handcuffs, but something else. Her heart pounded even harder and then the juice did force its way out of her throat, spraying the earth before her. With her hands behind her back, there was no way to wipe the sick from her mouth. Judgment upon her for her crime. Even while she wept from fear and dread, some freakishly alert portion of her brain noted that the man's grasp, while firm, was not angry or brutal, and he didn't wrench her arms painfully when he pulled them behind her.

A shameful part of her felt she deserved harsh treatment, expected it—perhaps would even have welcomed retribution. But the rest of her was pathetically grateful for small mercies. With a snuffling sob she tried to clear her nose. She turned her mouth against the shoulder of her shirt.

"Oh, for crying out loud." He took his weight from her leg and grabbed her arm just beneath her biceps to help her rise. "Get up." Abby could not hide her gasp, nor the wince that contorted her face when he gripped where Marsh had bruised her arm. "There's a picnic table. Sit on the bench, and keep your mouth shut." He hustled her over to the table constructed of concrete posts and bolted-on planks. "Stop that crying, too. You're well and truly busted, lady. Tears won't make me go easier on you. Now turn around and face the table." The man grasped her shoulder to balance her as Abby obeyed—the black mouth of the gun was pointed her way again, though the dog had backed off a few paces—and swung her legs over the bench. There would be no leaping up and running into the scrubby woods. He knew what he was doing, impeding her without physically restraining her beyond the cuffs.

He stood back from the table, lowering the gun at last. “What’s your name?”

Abby gulped and shook her head. She stared at the man. He wasn’t someone she knew from town. He didn’t recognize her, she could tell. She tried to think, but a moment later he spoke again.

“Mort, *fass*.” The dog bristled forward and pressed his nose against her again. Abby couldn’t stifle a fresh gasping sob.

“Your name.”

“I can explain—”

“I don’t want explanations. I want facts. Your name.”

Abby’s gaze dropped from the scar to the glinting barrel of the gun held at his side. Its latent menace dried her mouth, and try as she might, she could not summon enough moisture or breath to speak.

“Fine. We’ll do this your way.” He glowered at her and stepped forward. Abby flinched back instinctively, and then froze when the dog growled and breathed hot, moist air over her arm. She felt the prickle of his whiskers.

"I—I—" Fresh tears started. Abby feared they would only aggravate this man. "Please don't make him bite me."

"Then don't push me." He moved behind her and she craned her neck to watch him. "It'll be best if you stay still and don't give him a reason to attack. I'm going to take your wallet out of your pocket."

How odd. He's courteous, even when he's demanding information. His hand went smoothly into her pocket and withdrew the thin bifold wallet—Gary's, which she'd used since his funeral, a way to keep his memory alive.

The man put the table between them again. He laid the wallet on the plank surface and pulled out the contents one-handed. Her driver's license, the solitary credit card, photos, cash. Abby stared up at him, noting that the blood on his face was dried and smeared, but the cut in his hairline was still moist and fresh. It needed attention. She supposed her wild driving was the cause of his injury, and bit her lip. He'd been hurt because of her. He had close-cropped straw-colored hair and the tan of an outdoorsman. He was muscled and fit, and he handled the gun and the dog with familiar ease.

"Abigail McMurray. 302 Carson Street, Wildwood." His gaze flicked up and caught her own.

"Well, now, Abigail, what have you got to say for yourself?"

Abby swallowed hard and faced her own crime. "There isn't much to say, I guess. I stole your truck."

To her everlasting astonishment, the man threw back his head and laughed. She could tell it wasn't forced. He was honestly amused, and it startled her to see such confidence and poise in a man whose truck had been stolen, and who had the thief sitting right in front of him. She half expected the Phantom of the Opera to emerge from that awful visage, something rough-voiced and vengeful. The juxtaposition of the terrible scarring and his careful demeanor kept her off balance. "No kidding. I'd never have guessed if you hadn't told me. No, Abigail...what I want to know is *why.* What makes a soccer mom like you jump in a truck at a quickie mart and drive off? Where's your minivan, your Beemer? Start talking."

"I'm not a soccer mom. I'm a..." Abby's voice trailed off as she realized she'd just risen to his bait. She flushed. "Just call the cops and get it over with. I know I'm a felon."

He gestured around them. "Nice of you to confess, Abigail, but just where might there be a phone in these parts? I've checked my cell—there's no coverage here." He straightened, reached to tuck the gun into the back of his jeans, and then bent forward, knuckles on the table. "And if there's no cell coverage, that means we're pretty remote, doesn't it? No one to hear you scream when I make you tell me the truth. I'm more interested in the truth than in calling the cops."

No one to hear you scream. Don't grunt like that—what would the neighbors think? It's so hot outside. I don't want to wear a long-sleeved shirt to wash the car, but what would the neighbors think if they saw my arms? I'm not ready for those kinds of questions. I'll never be ready for those kinds of questions. If only Marsh wouldn't grip so hard. Abby pulled herself away from the dismaying flicker of memories. "I don't think I should talk without someone else here. A cop, or a lawyer. Someone."

"Your husband, maybe?" His fingers flicked Gary's license so that it spun toward her over the tabletop. She watched Gary's cheerful face come to a smiling stop. Who ever looked happy in their driver's license picture? Everyone else looked startled or stoned or fat, but Gary just looked like Gary, ordinary and plain until he smiled. "Is he going to meet you here, maybe?"

"He's dead." Why she felt compelled to say that much, Abby didn't know. She wedged her tongue between her teeth to remind herself to keep quiet. Sweat trickled down her face and the ridge of her spine.

"That explains why you're carrying a man's wallet and license." He gestured with his left hand, and the dog sat. Abby turned to look at it, expecting to see wild eyes and froth at its lips, and instead was startled by the lolling tongue as the dog panted in the day's glaring, humid heat. The shepherd looked as if he was grinning. He looked between Abby and the man continually, alert to each slight movement.

With the dog's muzzle away from her arm, Abby was able to relax the slightest bit. It was clear the dog would obey its master. She gained an odd respect for the man. He controlled the dog without force—or, rather, with only the force of his will. It was a concept she hadn't thought about for months. All men had been painted with Marsh's brush, despite the years spent basking in Gary's gentle love. One bad apple.

"Wait here. Don't try to run. My dog will stop you." The man went to the pickup and opened the passenger door, reaching in for the bag of groceries. He brought the sack to the table and started taking items out of it one by one. When he was finished, he surveyed the goods before him. The orange juice. Potato chips. Two cans of chili. A half gallon of milk. Grape jelly for Rosemary's sandwiches. Emergency rations because she hadn't had a chance to ask Marsh to drive her to the supermarket last evening.

Of course she hadn't. She'd been busy doing other things. Busy collecting the latest set of bruises on her arms, and elsewhere. Busy taking pills to knock back the pain. Busy wondering if this time he'd slip and mark her face. Her stomach clenched; how long would it be before Marsh came looking for her? Had he called the cops because he couldn't leave the day care while the clients were there? Or was he simply sitting, wondering what had happened to her, his anger growing? Had he fed the clients lunch?

Or…maybe… Marsh was afraid. Afraid she'd gone to the hospital or the cops at last. She hoped he was afraid, as terrified as she herself every time she saw the edges of his nostrils whiten or his hand reaching for her, or, what was worse, the look in his eye that signaled something less painful but more humiliating. She could picture him now, in one of his button-down short-sleeve shirts that brought out the green in his hazel eyes, watching her from where he sat in the living room while she folded his clothes—

"Did you steal these groceries? Was that why you were running away, because you were afraid someone at the store would catch you? Hardly seems worth the trouble for twenty bucks in junk food."

"I'm not a thief!" Abby flared, realizing how stupid that sounded when his eyebrows shot up and he looked at her with a gaze of blue disbelief and a twisted smirk on his well-cut mouth.

"Surely you're joking."

Abby bit her lip, mystified. Unless her perceptions had been skewed by the time spent with Marsh, the man was honestly amused. He was angry, too, but about the truck and not her responses. "I mean… I…had reasons why I…"

"Why you took my truck?" He came around the table and loomed over her. Abby shrank away as far as she could without losing her balance. It wasn't easy with her hands behind her back. "Come on, Abigail. Just give me the truth and this will go better for you. Why'd you steal my truck?"

"I'm sorry about that. Really, I am. It was a mistake, that's all. An error in judgment." She could hear herself babbling, and sought to divert him. "You're bleeding, did you know?"

"Your fault."

"I know. I'm sorry."

He tilted his head and studied her for a long moment. "You know, Abigail, I believe you are."

Marshall McMurray looked at his watch for the fifth time. What was taking Abigail so long? She hadn't managed to get herself to the grocery store last night, though she knew they needed several basic things to be able to serve the clients lunch. But even if she'd decided to buy more than the few critical items on the list Marsh had jotted, she should have come home from the corner store by now. It was only a few blocks away.

Marsh's gaze roved the large living room, where most of the people Abigail and Gary took into their home each day were playing board games. Rosemary, who should have been seated with Stephen playing checkers, was roaming the room looking for the television remote, which Marsh had in his pocket. She loved to get possession of the remote and blast the volume, hooting with excited glee when the others moaned in reaction. Abigail let her have it far too often. Marsh saw no need for such indulgence, not when it resulted in only more noise and agitation for the other people. He was in charge now; Gary was gone.

Marsh missed his brother, but he knew he was better suited to Abigail than Gary had been. Gary had always catered to Abigail's whims, which meant the business floundered. Small businesses, and women, required steady direction and a firm hand on the tiller. No wonder the adult day care hadn't been delivering much more than a basic living for his brother and his brother's wife. Together Marsh and Abigail would fix that, though. It wasn't Marsh's first choice for a living, but it was a start.

All the clients seemed quiet enough, but Marsh knew they'd be asking for Abigail before too much longer.

He went to the window and pulled aside the curtain that shielded the clients from the nosy stares of passersby and blocked some of the summer heat. The placement of the window didn't give him much of a view to the street, but Abigail wasn't walking up the driveway.

Behind Marsh, someone was slapping wet clay at the art table. Over and over. The flat sound reminded Marsh of the noise of skin on skin, the noise of two bodies in bed. And just like that, his brain revealed the explanation, the reason why Abigail hadn't come home yet.

She was meeting someone else.

His gut knotted. His fingers knotted in the fabric of the curtain, and he yanked it closed, sending the wooden rings rattling along the rod. Behind him the slapping continued. His fists wanted to knot, too.

She was probably sleeping with the man even now, leaving Marsh to deal with everything by himself, when she knew perfectly well state regulations required a minimum caregiver-to-patient ratio. She knew they were violating those very regulations, with only Marsh at hand to tend her clients. She knew it was nearly lunchtime when she left. She knew they'd be getting agitated, hungry and bored.

She'd told her clients she'd be right back.

Abigail had lied. Bald-faced lied. *Lied to him.*

Marsh turned from the window, glaring at Joe, the middle-aged man with pimples, who was slapping the clay mindlessly while he rocked back and forth in his chair, his eyes roving back and forth at high speed. Any moment now Joe would start moaning, overstimulated by whatever was going wrong in his neurons.

Abigail had left Marsh to cope with her pack of misfits, while she was off doing God knew what, probably with the idiot clerk at the store, maybe in the back room, maybe behind the store, up against the concrete wall where she could be seen from any passing car—

Rosemary bounced up to Marsh. "Lunchtime!"

Marsh gritted his teeth. "That's right. Almost lunchtime, as soon as Abigail comes back."

"I'm having peanut butter and grape jelly!" Rosemary said. Joe moaned a little, but Marsh could tell Rosemary's outburst had settled Joe in some way, opened a pressure valve. That was a good thing—Joe was damned strong, and without Abigail's soft voice and hands to calm him down, it would be a problem if Joe acted out his disturbance and became physical. Joe's eyes slowed their frantic flicking.

The old guy, Smith—Marsh never remembered his first name—who varied between utter stillness and manic activity, looked up. "Tuna fish. Tuna fish."

"Peanut butter!" Rosemary said, her mouth tightening as if Smith's preference would overrule her own.

Joe moaned again. His eyes started to flick.

Stephen joined the general ruckus, sending a hand across the checkerboard and scattering the game pieces. "Abby, Abby, where's Abby, where's lunch, where's Abby to make our lunch and pour the milk, lunch and milk, lunch and milk?"

Damnation, how all of them repeated themselves. It made Marsh nuts. If only he didn't have to put up with them—if only Abigail were here, as she should be. Next time he'd go and do the shopping, since she couldn't manage to get it right. Couldn't get herself home to feed the people she was responsible for.

"Shut up, Stephen!" Rosemary scrabbled after the checkers on the floor. "You messed me up. I was winning. You messed me up!"

Joe threw the pancake of clay at Rosemary, who shrieked in fury. Smith got out of his chair and started to walk in a circle in the center of the room, coming too close to Rosemary. Marsh was just in time to get between the two of them before Rosemary decided to slap.

"I know what, we'll all have popcorn for lunch!" Marsh said, with false cheer. He cursed Abigail silently. She had a lesson coming when she did get home, after causing all this mess. "Let's go in the kitchen and put a bag in the microwave. It'll be special, real special." Just like the special words he'd have for Abigail later that night, once everyone had gone home to their families.

"Special," repeated Joe, getting to his feet.

"And a movie. I get to pick!" Rosemary chanted. She stepped on the pancake of clay and ground it into the short-loop carpet. Marsh closed his eyes for a second, not nearly long enough to count to ten, but enough to allow him to ignore the newest mess. Then he got hold of Smith by his elbow and brought him along to the kitchen. The only way to stop Smith from walking in circles for the rest of the day was to completely change the scenery and give him a new focus. No way was Marsh going to let Rosemary pick the movie, though. He was damned sick of *Finding Nemo,* her latest favorite.

The afternoon wore on, full of countless exhausting and infuriating outbursts from the entire group. Marsh's patience thinned with each passing minute that Abigail didn't arrive. Rosemary and Stephen both had meltdowns ending in tears and thrown objects, events that wouldn't have happened had Abigail been present instead of shirking her responsibilities, wherever the hell she'd gone.

Marsh couldn't shake the idea that she was with another man. Where would she have met someone else? The produce aisle at the grocery store? It wasn't like Abigail went very many places without Marsh. He could hardly think. He tried to keep himself from going to the window every few minutes, because the clients were starting to notice his own agitation. He popped more bags of popcorn and got out crackers and cheese, and settled the group for a long afternoon of movie watching. It was easier than doing art projects or baking cookies in the kitchen, though both activities were favorites with the group.

Finally, at four in the afternoon, just ninety minutes before family members were due to retrieve their grown-up children, Marsh dug out the telephone book and wetted his finger to flip through the yellow pages. God help Abigail if she was still at that store.

Marsh dialed, keeping an eye on the group, who were quiet at the moment, engrossed in the umpteenth repeat of *Finding Nemo.* Stupid film.

When someone answered on the third ring, Marsh had to swallow down a growl of anger. "I'm looking for someone who was headed to your store a little while ago. I…uh, forgot to tell her to get a gallon of milk. She's about five feet six, and she has a long light brown ponytail. Wearing jeans and a blue cotton shirt. Is she there?"

"Store's empty, just me here right now."

"Has she been there?"

"Not since I came on shift."

"Well, when was that?" Marsh couldn't believe the idiocy of the clerk.

"Coupla hours ago. Look, is there a problem?"

"No. There's no problem. Is anyone else there, your supervisor maybe, someone who was there before you?"

"No, man. Wish I could help you, but like I said, haven't seen her."

"Thanks." *Liar. You're probably the man she's run off to meet. She's probably there now, listening to you answer my questions, laughing at me.* Marsh clicked off and put the handset away, in the cupboard, where it was out of Rosemary's view. That woman had a real thing for anything with buttons on it, telephones, remotes, controls for electric blankets, stereos.

"Where's Abby?" Smith asked.

Marsh clenched his fists behind his back. "She's… She had to go to the doctor." Yes, that was it. Get the story squared away with the clients, then set the expectations with their families: no day care tomorrow, Abigail was ill, it was probably contagious, she'd been at the doctor all day. Really sorry for the inconvenience and no notice. Knew they'd understand. Really, really sorry.

Beside Smith, Joe started to rock and hit his hand on his thigh. "Don't like the doctor. Don't like the doctor."

"She'll be fine," Marsh assured him, putting

a big hand on Joe's shoulder. "It's just a virus. In a day or so everything will be back to normal."

"Don't like the doctor," Joe repeated, but his voice was quieter as long as Marsh was touching him. Abigail was going to need the doctor when Marsh got through with her, that much was certain. He'd make sure her legs were too sore to carry her off to the store, hell, go anywhere.

"She'll get some medicine and be fine."

Smith turned his head and looked up at Marsh. "I don't like it when Abby isn't here."

"I don't like you," Rosemary chimed in. "I think you're mean."

"Now, now," Marsh muttered. "That's not very nice, Rosie. I think we'll have to tell your families you can't come here tomorrow, since Abigail won't be feeling very well. We don't want you to catch her virus, do we?"

"Mean," said Rosemary, and Smith nodded, then kept nodding. Well, Smith could nod his head right off his neck, for all Marsh cared. He wouldn't stop the perseveration this time.

"Shut up and watch the movie. All of you. Or I'll turn it off, and you can just sit in your chairs until it's time to go. You don't want that, do you?"

Joe began to rock again. Idiots, all of them. Why Abigail thought they were worth bothering with, Marsh would never understand. When all of their faces were turned back to the neurotic fish-father searching for his lost fish-son on the television, Marsh walked into the next room to get his temper under control and plan what he needed to say to the families to keep them away tomorrow. He couldn't legally operate without a second certified attendant, but more important, he didn't want to.

He'd see to it that Abigail learned this lesson. Learned it well. Learned it pronto. She'd never leave him in the lurch like this again.

And she'd never get another chance to sneak off with someone while Marsh wasn't looking.

Ever.

While he took the bag of groceries back to the truck, Cade assessed what he knew about the woman seated at the picnic table.

Thirty-one years old, based on her driver's license. She was too thin in that nervous way of women who were perpetually on their guard, either out of fear that if they gained weight their lovers would abandon them, or anxiety for other reasons. He was betting on the latter. His cop instincts were telling him something much bigger than a shallow boyfriend was at work here. You didn't steal a truck because you were anxious about gaining a little weight from too many chocolates or not enough exercise. It was possible her thinness was from drugs, but her teeth weren't those of a meth-freak, rotting and ground down.

Until he knew for certain, he'd be cautious and expect the worst.

Her face and hands were tanned, but at the gaping shirt neck where a button was missing, he could see pale flesh beneath. Above her wrists the flesh was pale, as well. So she got out in the sun but not in short sleeves. Her straight hair was light brown, edging past her shoulders but scraped back in a plain ponytail, with blonder streaks threading through it. He'd have bet money the streaks were from the sun and not a bottle.

Her shirt and jeans were worn. Maybe she'd been doing chores when she decided to take his truck on a joyride, or maybe she couldn't afford new things.

The groceries looked like lunch for someone. Herself? Did women buy chili for themselves? Potato chips, sure, as an indulgence or, as a few of his girlfriends had taught him, greasy burnt offerings for the PMS monster. But why shop at a convenience store, where prices were guaranteed to be high? Simple: because she didn't have a car, and the store was closest to where she lived. She'd driven before, though—you couldn't just steal a manual transmission vehicle without knowing how to drive a stick. She'd never have made it out of the parking lot, much less to a campground in the middle of nowhere an hour from town.

Her husband was dead. That lined up with the

bare left hand, and perhaps the worn clothing, but not that nagging hum in the back of his head that told him this woman was terrified of more than just his anger at her theft of his property.

This woman was running away from something. When she looked up at him as he loomed over her, he saw the flicker of alarm in her gray eyes. Her straight, level light brown eyebrows were drawn together over her nose in a worried expression. She feared him, feared his reaction to her crime. As well she should—but Cade knew this woman was no hardened criminal, just a woman on the run. Now, to get her to give up her secrets, because he was sure there was a doozy lurking just beneath the surface, like a catfish in a murky lake.

"Why stop here?" Cade questioned, leaning too close. Intimidation often worked to jolt confessions out of honest people. Habitual liars were a different matter. They'd learned to sidle along the truth for maximum believability, but he didn't think this woman was a liar. A little judicious pressure would get him what he sought. "Middle of nowhere. How does a chick like you drive my beater truck to a campground? How'd you even know this place was here, much less drive straight to it?"

"I've… I've been here before. Fishing. Years ago."

"You're on a fishing trip, are you? Saw my truck, thought it would be just the thing for a little jaunt? Who are you meeting here? When do they arrive?"

"No, I— That's not how it is. I'm not meeting—" She flushed darkly and stopped. "You're trying to make me talk. Just call the police and be done with it. You have all the proof you need. My fingerprints are all over the cab of your truck. I won't even try to deny it."

"That's right, I'm trying to make you talk. I don't think it's unreasonable of me to want to understand this, do you? If the police get involved, I may never learn the whole story."

She narrowed her eyes at him speculatively, her soft mouth tightening. "Are you…are you saying that if I tell you everything, you might not…might not call the police?"

Was that hope in her voice? Cade felt only mild guilt at using law enforcement interrogation techniques on this woman, who every passing minute seemed less and less a criminal and more and more a runaway girlfriend.

"Whadd'ya know, I think maybe I am. Why don't you see if you can convince me not to truss you up, toss you in the back of my truck and haul you to the nearest sheriff's department? I'm not an unreasonable man. Maybe I won't bother with the cops. Maybe you'll get a pass. But your story's got to be good, and I've got to believe it."

Abigail sat there, considering, for nearly a

minute. Then she looked up at him. “I stole your truck because I needed to get away from some bad things in my personal life. I know it was wrong. I would rather not go into them, but I can at least promise you they’re not illegal things. I’m really not a criminal. I’m just…stupid, I guess.”

Cade folded his arms. “Not good enough, Abigail. I don’t buy the stupid part.” He looked up at the sun. “But we’ve got all afternoon. You say this is a good fishing spot? Maybe I’ll just see about that. What’s biting, do you think? Some bream?”

She nodded, her winged brows drawing together above her nose, revealing her confusion. “Maybe bream. That’s a tributary of the Styx River, and there’ll be bluegill or sunfish. Catfish, too, if you like those. Lake fish, mostly, here where the current is slow.”

Cade put a foot up on the bench and leaned his elbow on his knee. His hand dangled, not carelessly, but not aggressively. Her eyes went to it briefly, checking it as he suspected she would. Then her eyes returned to wander to the side of his face, where the acid had ravaged his skin, marking him as a monster, a beast, a savage. “Styx, huh? I just can’t get over how many backwoods Florida places have these scholarly names. I’m not much for catfish, unless they’re farm-raised. Taste too much like mud, otherwise.”

“They say you are what you eat—I suppose that

goes for fish, too." She lifted her chin to gesture at the unscarred side of his face. "You're still bleeding a little."

"Go on about stealing the truck, Abigail."

"Someone should look at the injury. It's swollen like a goose egg. You're not feeling dizzy, are you?"

"You're avoiding answering my questions. While you think about what you want to tell me, I'm just gonna do a little fishing. Don't try to leave the table. Mort will stop you." He strode to the truck, conscious that she turned her head and body to watch him. It wasn't exactly kind to leave her sitting in the hot sun while he sat in the relative cool of the shaded riverbank, but it might be the thing that pried her story out of her.

Cade didn't really plan to fish, but he'd make a good show of it. And if a bream or perch or bluegill turned up, so much the better. He just might be in a mood for some fresh fish. There was charcoal in the back of the truck, and a handy metal grill rested on a concrete fire circle not far from the picnic table. He checked the pistol's safety and returned the Beretta to his waistband. Opening the truck's hatch, he reached inside for a camp stool and his fishing tackle.

As he walked past the table with his gear, Abigail spoke. "Since your dog will watch me and there's nowhere for me to go, could you please take these off?" She lifted her wrists away from her back to remind him of the cable ties he'd cuffed her with. "They're really uncomfortable." Her movements strained the front of her worn chambray shirt and hinted at the womanly shape of her beneath. Her throat was flushed with heat and dewy with perspiration, the cords of her neck trim and taut.

Cade looked at her thoughtfully and said, "No." He turned his back and found a spot on the riverbank where Abigail was in easy view and he could cast into the slow-flowing stream. He set up the stool and sat at an angle. Mort looked at him alertly, but Cade gave the hand signal to continue on guard, and the shepherd turned his brown eyes back to Abigail.

Abigail shifted, trying to make herself comfortable on the hard bench seat of the picnic table. The movement made Cade wonder what she looked like in motion, walking, bending, busy at whatever it was she did for a living. He forced his gaze toward the river for a few minutes, working at clearing his head. Normally his emotions didn't get this involved with the people he was investigating, or worse yet, taking into custody. He had to get his priorities back in order. Her problems weren't his. Intellectually he knew that, but he continued to feel a strong need to dig out the truth. It wasn't a rational need. He told himself he was off duty, on vacation, but it didn't make even a dent in his stubborn will.

She was just a woman with a problem. He'd seen hundreds of them, helped some, condemned others. He didn't have to fix the world. Hell, she probably didn't even want him in her business in the first place, but by stealing his truck she'd dragged him right into her mess.

What would she look like if she smiled? Would the smile reach her eyes, transform her from sadly pretty to beautiful? Or would she get a goofy grin on her face that made her more charming than pretty? What would it be like to be the man Abigail McMurray smiled at? He missed being the sort of man women looked at with interest, even pleasure. The scar on his face saw to that.

Cade shook his head again, continuing to gaze at the river so Abigail would not see him scowling. When he scowled, he was truly a monster. He was unaccountably unwilling for her to view him that way. He might be ugly—he couldn't help that—but he didn't have to be frightening.

She stole your truck, Latimer. Keep that in mind. He tried to summon his cop brain uppermost, but it was having trouble, fighting with the white knight living deep within. The two sides of himself weren't always incompatible, but in this case he wasn't merely a disinterested party. He was personally involved, and growing more so by the minute. The cop brain had made him one of the best at the undercover game. It was the knight that made him keep believing in the basic goodness and worth of most people. Some people were worth saving, and his instincts told him Abigail might be one of them.

He fought down the urge to whack his own forehead with his open palm. He was acting like an idiot, thinking with his hormones instead of his brain. Abigail was pretty, sure. She was ragged and worn with care and fright. Likely he'd never have a chance with her, and he shouldn't want one. She probably wasn't the sort of woman who'd date a deputy for any reason, even if he weren't ugly as sin these days. He hadn't had the best of luck in the past with women, at least the sort of women who might want a long-term relationship. It took only one or two late nights on duty, a missed date at a swanky restaurant or a story about a dangerous takedown and a gunshot blessedly gone wide, for a woman to decide she was better off without the worry and fear her man might not come home some night. There were moments when he himself had wondered if scratching the adrenaline itch was worth it, if he might not find similar satisfaction in some other job where his life wasn't on the line half the time. Maybe then a woman would find him a worthy recipient of her time and affection. Those kinds of women weren't out stealing trucks, however. They were making vastly different life choices.

He knew all that.

It didn't make a difference.

Cade reeled in the lure and tossed it again. If only getting crooks to take bait was as easy as getting a fish to bite. Some of them were too smart, like this one. He stole a glance over his shoulder.

Abigail was still seated like a good girl, her head drooping, staring at the picnic table's wood grain. The sun blazed down on her head, turning the paler streaks in her brown hair to blazing gold. Even confined in a ponytail, it was the sort of hair that would look gorgeous loose around her shoulders, alive with gleaming highlights as it fell forward along her cheeks.

Chapter 3

Abby sat at the table, hands behind her back, sweating in the sauna heat of the humid sky. The table was out in the sun, and the sweet black shade of the nearby moss-hung oaks taunted her.

What had just happened here? She would have sworn the man had started off in a murderous fury, having every intention of packing her off to the police. Somewhere in his interrogation of her the tone had subtly shifted from one of anger to one of curiosity.

She eyed him where he perched on the incongruously small stool and leaned his back against one of the tall cypress knees that jutted from the river's edge. His fishing line trailed lazily in the slow-flowing water, and every few minutes he reeled it in and flicked it back upstream to float past again.

He sat with the scarred side of his face toward her. Now she had the leisure to study it, and reflect on some of her limited nursing training, the few years she'd had before taking a professional course designed to focus on adult day care in support of the business. It looked like a chemical burn of some sort, raised and raw-looking, ropy and rough in places, shiny and slick in others. The outer end of his left eyebrow was missing, giving him a somewhat quizzical appearance. He was fortunate that the worst of the chemicals had missed his eye. Even from a distance she could see his thick sandy lashes, which gave his startling blue eyes a deceptively sleepy look.

His T-shirt fit him closely, limning muscles in his arms and chest and showcasing his flat belly between the open lapels of his fishing vest. With the single exception of the scar, he was a man she would have turned to watch on a street. Lean and strong, hair that was more gold than brown, tall. He had a way of moving that spoke of ease and friendliness, until his eyes caught those of an observer and the wariness surfaced. His voice, once the anger had drained away, was quiet and firm with only a slight trace of a Southern accent in the vowels.

She had liked his laugh.

Abby frowned at this thought. Overthinking this man's general attractiveness was beyond pointless. Shortly he would tire of waiting for her to talk. He would shut her in the back of his truck and haul her off to the county sheriff. He had every right to do it.

She wondered if the lawmen would give her a break if she showed them her bruises and filed charges against Marsh. It wasn't the first time she'd fantasized about reporting Marsh's various crimes. She was pretty sure she could make an assault charge stick, and maybe even domestic abuse. But it would mean facing him down in public, and he was so far inside her guard that he knew every last secret, every weakness. He had pried up the edges of all her insecurities and peered beneath to where her doubts and fears lurked, and he had magnified them.

The telephone rang at all hours. It was a comfort knowing he thought about her, even at six in the morning or eleven at night.

"How was the day? Got any good stories for me, Abigail?"

"Oh...nothing fun. Just the usual grind. And messes. Sam had a bad seizure, so I had to call the ambulance, which upset everyone else. Rosemary cried and broke her soup bowl. Tomato soup everywhere. The new girl from the agency is still

getting the hang of things, so most of the work is on me."

"Ah, Abigail, honey. I'm so sorry. Tomorrow will be better, I'm sure. In fact, I'll guarantee it for you."

"Thanks, Marsh. I know you can't do anything from there, but it's just so good to hear a friendly voice. Someone who understands."

"Have you got any of that merlot I bought you left?"

"A little." Smiling to herself now, picturing his charming grin and the way the cork had resisted him when he opened that first bottle and they'd toasted Gary's picture on the mantelpiece the night of the funeral. Two shared bottles and a crying jag later, she'd fallen asleep on his shoulder with his arm around her and the light cotton throw from the back of the sofa drawn across them both.

Or a wake-up call, when she was drowsy and unguarded, warm with sleep and alone in a bed meant for two people.

"Hey, there...how's my gray-eyed sister-in-law this fine morning?"

"It's raining here."

"I didn't catch you last night—I called a couple times but you didn't answer. Were you out?"

"Yeah...what time is it?"

"Still early. You've got time to get a little more

shut-eye, but I wanted to say hello before I have to start my commute. Were you out with Judy?"

"Yeah. She made me go dancing with her and her hubby. Said I needed a little smoky air and loud music."

"Abigail...it's too soon for that."

"I know. I came home early."

"I wish I was there with you."

"Me, too."

As the weeks after the funeral dragged on, she began changing her schedule to be home when she thought Marsh might call. She told friends she was fine, just tired.

Abby wrenched her mind back again. She had to focus, and try to relax. Her left shoulder was cramping, and she rotated it slowly as far as she was able with her wrists behind her. She kept one eye on the dog, hoping that none of her movements would be interpreted as aggression and trigger a reaction. Dogs had never frightened her, but she had a healthy respect for this one's teeth and intelligence and exceptional training.

Even more than respecting the dog, she respected his owner. That brought a question to mind. What did a man like him need with this sort of dog? What line of work was he in? Abby traced along this path like a bloodhound on a scent. He carried a gun, he knew how to secure a criminal—

for criminal she was, like it or not—and he had a well-trained police dog at his command.

The question popped out before she could stop it. "Are *you* a cop?"

She thought he stiffened, but he did not turn and she couldn't be certain. "Why do you ask?"

"It would explain a few things."

"As I keep telling you, you're the one who needs to do the explaining. Have you thought about that a little more?" Lazily he reeled in the line, flicked it back out into the river, the reel whirring and the lure landing with a faint plop. Abby watched the rings ripple out and dwindle, erased by the flow of the tea-brown water.

"There's just…really, nothing to explain. I've told you the truth. I'm running from some personal things and lost my head."

"You keep saying that, but I'm like those TV junkies who sit home staring at the Hollywood gossip shows. I want the dirt."

Despite herself a rueful laugh forced its way past her lips. "What I wouldn't give to be back at home staring at the TV." Even reminding Rosemary to share the television remote would be better than the stomach-roiling anxiety she was feeling now. It was hard to decide which was worse: the fear she'd be arrested and jailed for what she'd done, or the certain nightmare when Marsh caught up with her.

"I guess it would be better if you hadn't started down this road, huh, Abigail?"

"No kidding." She fell silent. Sweat trickled down her spine, making her itch as it went. She wondered if she was flexible enough to wriggle backward through the circle of her arms and bring her wrists in front of her. The man would probably stop her if she became too active. A droning sweat bee began to show interest in the moist skin of her neck, and there was nothing she could do about it except toss her head and hope her ponytail knocked the insect away.

"Something wrong?" Was that humor in his voice?

"Nothing a good toxic cloud of pesticide wouldn't fix."

Now it was a definite chuckle. "You're doing it to yourself, you know. Dish a little dirt, Abigail."

"I don't even know your name."

"What, you didn't go through my glove compartment and steal my registration?"

Abby scrubbed her face against her shoulder. The sweat was getting into her eyes, stinging with salt. "No," she mumbled. "I think your dog needs a drink of water."

At this comment, the man did turn. He looked with concern at the shepherd, and then nodded. "Wouldn't hurt. I was getting him a drink when you so rudely interrupted us in that parking lot by stealing my truck." He propped his fishing pole against a nearby scrub oak and returned to the truck, where he took a bottle of water from the back, and a blue plastic bowl, and proceeded to pour the bottled water in the bowl for the dog. Abby found herself swallowing reflexively, and with a gleam in his bright blue eyes the man spoke.

"Cade Latimer. And this is Mort."

"Pleased to meet you, Mr. Latimer." She was afraid that the words would come out sarcastically, but instead she was speaking the truth, to her own astonishment. Under any other circumstances she'd have enjoyed talking to this man. "He's a beautiful dog." She watched as Latimer cued the dog off guard and permitted him to drink his fill.

"Thanks. You look thirsty, too." He tipped his head back, bottle to his lips, and drank down what little he hadn't poured into the bowl. His muscular throat gleamed with a light film of sweat. "But maybe your stomach's still unsettled from the rough ride. Or the poor company. Your skin is pasty-looking."

Now that he was closer to her again, Abby could see that the cut was still seeping, though slowly. He had smeared blood over the side of his face each time he wiped at the cut. It looked sore, and the little bit of nursing training she had made her fingers itch to tend the wound. "I'm not thirsty just now. Mr. Latimer, that cut really does need attention. I can see to that for you. It needs cleaning and some antibiotic cream. It might even need stitches."

He slanted a bright blue glance at her. "How do I know you won't take advantage of the situation and incapacitate me?"

Now Abby did laugh, the corner of her mouth curling up in a rueful smile. "I'm a thief, not a murderer. I did the damage, I'll clean up after it. I may not want to tell you all the gory details of my life, but I'm an honorable woman."

His smile, when it came, transformed him. "Damned if I don't believe you, Abigail. All right. Sit tight while I dig out the first aid kit, then I'll clip the cable ties so you can use your hands."

Abby watched Cade Latimer stretch over the tailgate and emerge with a small blue canvas kit with a red cross silk-screened on it. He brought it to the table and opened it.

"Some more of that bottled water would be good," Abby suggested.

"I thought you weren't thirsty."

"For cleaning the cut."

Cade nodded and returned with two more bottles of water. He twisted open both and set them near her. He stood very close to her and reached out to cup her chin and turn her face toward him. Abby met his gaze, startled anew by how very blue his eyes were. The work-roughened skin of his palm rasped her jawline and she swallowed, trying not to gulp.

"Understand me, Abigail McMurray. I'm going to let you loose so you can clean up this cut, but make one false move and I won't hesitate to stop you. It may be as simple as twisting an arm behind your back, or it might be Mort's teeth in your leg."

Or a bullet from your gun. She couldn't look away. The blue of his eyes was intense. A rim of darker blue edged the iris as if to keep the liquid color contained, and different shades of blue rayed from the pupil like spokes in a wheel. His eyes were so arresting she began to lose track of the conversation.

"Show me you understand."

"I don't understand what you want, Marsh."

"What's to understand? Didn't you do as much for Gary? C'mon. I know he was a boob man. He always was, from the time we were kids." Marsh's hands trembled as he grasped her shoulders, and Abby could tell his hands wanted to slide down, over the breasts he'd just complimented.

"I just want to see your breasts," he said. "Maybe touch them a little. Gary always said you had beautiful breasts. A little more than a handful, and sweet."

"Gary never talked to you about my breasts!" She didn't know what shocked her more—that Marsh wanted her to show him her naked breasts,

or the idea that Gary had talked to Marsh about something so personal. "Our sex life is—was—private."

"He was my brother. He told me a lot of things that would surprise you."

"What else did he tell you?" Abby gasped, clutching at the front of her shirt as if the buttons might fly off by the force of Marsh's hungry gaze alone.

"He told me you're the sweetest bit of tail a man could wish for. He told me you're generous, and a little shy, and kind of prudish until you've had a little wine."

Prudish? Abby stared at Marsh, her mouth dropping open. Tail?

When he reached out and tucked her tumbled hair behind her ears, she didn't stop him. He leaned his forehead against hers and spoke sweetly, reminding her how much help he was around the place. He told her how much he missed Gary. When his fingertip touched the hollow of her throat and traced her collarbone, she didn't stop him. He told her grief had made her slimmer and more beautiful than ever. He talked about the projects he had in mind, how simple it would be to build a ramp out the back door to the patio for their wheelchair clients.

When he unbuttoned her shirt and smoothed the lapels back against the fabric, she didn't stop him.

And when, a little later, he straddled her, holding her down on the living room floor with his knees planted at her elbows in a promise of pain if she fought, and his hands pressing her breasts together while his hips pistoned his humid, naked penis between them, she couldn't *stop him.*

Marsh's silver Honda sedan started immediately when he turned the key. He adjusted the seat backward an inch. Abigail hadn't slid it back where it belonged last time she'd driven the car. Her list of sins was long, and getting longer as the day dragged into evening. Marsh backed out of the driveway, now that the last of the clients and their families were gone.

They wouldn't be back in the morning, either. He'd bought himself a day with the story of Abigail's contagious virus—a stomach virus, he'd explained to the families, lots of vomiting, the doctor would want her to rest and hydrate, give her body a chance to recover, certainly they were too professional to expose the clients to such a virulent ailment.

She'd need every moment of that recovery time when he was finished with her, Marsh thought furiously, spinning the Honda's steering wheel and guiding the sedan swiftly around the corner. It was only a few blocks to the convenience store. He could have walked there in the time it would take to drive and park again, but he had a sinking feeling he'd be chasing Abigail all over town half the night.

At the convenience store, he parked by the front door and waited, engine idling quietly, watching a few customers come and go. He didn't see Abigail inside, and the clerk at the register was a woman, not the idiot he'd spoken to earlier. Even better; he preferred to talk to women, anyway. When the last customer drove away, Marsh went inside.

He scanned the aisles quickly on his way to the refrigerator wall at the back, where he selected a soda and took it up to the register. Abigail wasn't crouching behind a display or sitting in one of the booths in the café area near the coffee stand and fountain drinks.

"Hey," said the clerk, smiling.

"Hey, yourself," Marsh replied with a big grin. She was a cute little number, a bit long in the tooth, but she took care of herself. No dark roots in the blond hair, though it was teased too high for his personal preference. Not too much makeup, except where her mascara clumped. Her top fit her body nicely without looking trashy. "Hope it's been a good one for you. You must be about to head home to your hubby and a good dinner."

She laughed and turned his soda around to show the barcode to the reader. "Not me, no. Hubby's long gone to hell or Arizona, I don't care which, not that I could tell the difference. Got a while left on shift, too."

Marsh fished slowly in his wallet, buying time while he thought about how to get the information he wanted from her. "A shame, great-looking gal like you."

"Well, hey, thanks." Her cheeks went pink, just a little, and Marsh smiled even wider.

"But speaking of great-looking gals, I was wondering if my own gal's been here. She's late getting home. I figured I'd swing by her work and give her a ride home, but they said she left a while ago. Sometimes she stops off here on her way home. Seen her? I hate to sound like a worrywart, but you know how it is."

The clerk shot her hip to the right and gave him another smile. "Least someone cares about her, right? What's she look like?"

"She's got long brown hair. She likes to wear it in a ponytail. Probably in jeans and a blue shirt, if she just got off work. Big gray eyes. Bet she looks tired, too."

The woman thought for a moment, took the five he held out and pursed her lips. "I don't think I've seen her."

"Maybe it was before your shift, then. Is the other guy still here? Maybe I could talk to him, too." Get a real good look at the jerk who'd had his hands all over Abigail. Unbuttoning her shirt.

Letting down her hair. Touching things that didn't belong to him.

He hadn't said it just right, or maybe he didn't have his face blank enough. Either way, Marsh knew the moment he'd lost the connection. She straightened up and gave him a long, cool stare before counting out his change. She put it on the counter between them instead of putting it into his hand. She closed the cash drawer, and then took a step back. "He's not here," she said slowly. "Tell you what, why don't you leave your phone number, and I'll mention you stopped in. He can call you, maybe."

Marsh pasted a smile on his face again. "That's okay. She's probably just taking the scenic route. She likes the park. I'll try her there. Thanks for your help." *Thanks for nothing.*

"Sure you don't want to leave your number?" She pushed a pad of paper and a pen toward him.

So you can give it to the cops? Think I'm stupid? Marsh shook his head and took his change and his soda. "Thanks, anyway. I'm sure she's just stopped at a friend's or something like that. I'm sure I'm worrying for nothing." He tried another smile, but it felt false on his face. He lifted the soda bottle in a cheery toast and kept his stride even, pace calm. Not a worried man, no. No reason to be worried.

The Honda started right up, as always. But Marsh looked at the glass front of the convenience store, where the clerk stood looking out at him, a pen and a pad of paper in hand.

"You'd better not be writing down my license plate number, bitch," he muttered under his breath, fighting the urge to screech the Honda out of the parking lot and into the street with the accelerator pressed to the floor. His heart gave a thud at the idea of the cops showing up at his house, asking about a woman who hadn't come home from work. A check on Abigail's welfare. For the first time the chance of Abigail reporting him to the cops seemed possible. Always before now he'd had her within arm's reach, where he could talk her around, explain to her how things worked, how crazy she made him. Crazy with love and desperate to keep her. He'd given up his life in Jacksonville to move to this pissant town, all because Abigail was here.

God, he loved her. Now she was his, the way she should have been from the start, before Gary somehow got between them. Marsh had seen her first, but it was Gary who'd managed to hook her, and Marsh had never figured out how that had happened. Somewhere between one bottle of beer at a neighborhood barbecue and the next, Abigail was laughing at Gary's stupid jokes and sitting next to him on the edge of her cousin's swimming pool. Marsh could still see her long tanned legs dangling in the water, the skirt of her sundress above her knees to keep it from getting wet. Then she and Gary started dating, going for long walks and dinners, having heart-to-heart talks that didn't include Marsh.

Marsh would find her; he had to. He hadn't worked this hard only to have her run away.

Thinking about the barbecue reminded him of the most logical place to look: Judy and Drew's house. They were easily a mile away, but Abigail had had all afternoon to walk there. If she was anywhere, she would be at her best friend's house.

Marsh slowed to a stop at the next corner, got his bearings and headed north, thinking all the while about the first time Abigail had taken him to Judy and Drew's for a barbecue, not all that long after they'd put Gary in the ground. He replayed the evening in his mind.

"Turn left?" Marsh had asked.

"Yes. Judy and Drew live in that blue house—right here."

"Where is it you know Judy from, again?" Marsh guided the Honda to the curb. It was quiet and sweet in the cabin of the car, with Abigail in the passenger seat. Sweet, so sweet. He liked when their elbows brushed, liked the way her light perfume fragranced each breath he took.

"She used to help me and Gary out sometimes, when we first opened the day care."

"Oh, yeah. What's Drew do?"

"He's a mechanic. Got his own shop."

Marsh and Abigail had been out to dinner a few times in the past couple of months, but this was the first time any of her friends would meet him since Gary's funeral. They stood by the car a moment. Abigail must have noticed him biting his lower lip, because she spoke softly as she came around the back of the car.

"What's up, Marsh?"

"I was just wondering if we turned off the iron. Maybe we should go back and check." He really wasn't in a party mood; he would rather be back at Gary's—Abigail's—house, having a quiet dinner in the kitchen, and maybe some television after. They'd sit on the sofa, only a foot or so apart. Where he could touch her, if he wanted.

"It shuts itself off after a few minutes. Gary was so forgetful, it was easier to buy one that remembered for him."

He nodded, reaching into the backseat for the fruit salad they'd brought for the potluck. Abigail touched his arm. "They liked Gary. They'll like you."

"I'm not Gary."

Abigail was clearly touched by his insecurity. Her smile was gentle and understanding. "Just stick close to me, then."

The party was on Drew and Judy's big patio in the backyard. Marsh was friendly to others, but attentive to Abigail, bringing her drinks and surprising her with a filled plate from the buffet table as she sat talking with one of Judy's neighbors. He stood behind her and reached for an occasional nibble.

"You know, they'll let you have your own plate, Marsh."

"Yours tastes better." Marsh laughed. The neighbor smiled at their banter. They were a couple, weren't they? It was apparent to others already.

Yes, he thought now. *That's where Abigail will be. Having coffee, getting sympathy from that bitch Judy, telling lies about me to explain why she isn't home tending to her business.*

He parked and got out of the car. It was time for Abigail to come home, where she belonged. His fists clenched at his sides and he shook them out, bouncing a little on the balls of his feet, loosening up, before he strode up the walkway to the little blue house. He couldn't arrive at the door angry. Drew was probably there.

Halfway to the door, Marsh turned around, went back to the car and drove around the corner before turning in a neighbor's driveway and driving slowly back, to park two houses down. He turned off the engine and the lights, and simply watched. Drew might be there, and he'd certainly understand Marsh's desire to have Abigail back at home where she belonged, but maybe Marsh would have a chance to see for himself just how traitorous Abigail had become.

Because what if…just maybe… Drew was the man Abigail had run off with?

Marsh sat in the early twilight, strong fingers drumming on the steering wheel, watching Drew and Judy's house. Thinking.

Planning.

"Abigail? Do you understand me?" Cade asked her a second time for agreement, looking into her cloudy gray eyes. Though she was meeting his gaze, she was far away in her thoughts, and they weren't happy ones, judging from the faint vertical line between her silky brows, and the tightness of her lips. Strands of her hair had escaped her ponytail and were sticking to the sides of her face and her neck. Cade knew a sudden urge to lift them away and put them back where they belonged, or to loose her hair entirely, watch it catch the bright light.

At last she nodded. "I won't try anything stupid. Promise."

"Good." He released her, moved behind her and used the short, thick blade of his pocketknife to cut the cable ties that served as impromptu handcuffs. The skin of her wrists was reddened where she had strained against the bonds, but unbroken, and not bruised. It was velvety soft where he touched it, slightly moist with sweat. He watched her shoulders slump in relief at the release of tension. She massaged her wrists and shoulders briefly before standing to examine the contents of the first aid kit.

"Sit down," she told him, adding "please" when he raised an eyebrow at her. He sat with his back away from her, so she'd have to reach around him to get to the gun, jammed tight in the back of his waistband. He gestured to Mort to wait not far away. The dog retreated to a blob of dark shade under a nearby scrub oak, and turned to face them.

"He's got the right idea." Abigail nodded toward the dog, opening a package of gauze pads and wetting two. "It's really hot out here. Shade would be nice. I'm going to wash the area of the cut. Speak up if what I'm doing hurts."

Cade felt her slim fingers probing at the wound, assessing the shape and size of the goose egg. Then came the welcome cool of the wet cotton, soaking first, and then gently swabbing away blood from his hair and skin. He sat alert, though it was more for show than need. She seemed absorbed in her task, dabbing, remoistening the pads and setting them aside as they became red with his blood. She was close enough that he could smell her skin, acrid with leftover fear and adrenaline, perspiration, an undertone of soap. She moved his head from one position to the next like someone who was comfortable touching others. An image of Abigail mending the cuts and scrapes of a child snagged in the screen of his mind. The abruptness of the thought and his vague, negative reaction to it startled him.

I hope I'm not keeping her away from her kids. But then, if there are kids at home, maybe they're the reason she left. Sometimes they get to be too much. I don't think I ever want kids. He knew she was widowed, but how many people were in her family? The urge to know the answer was too strong, so he began to lead her to an answer.

"You seem like a pro at this first aid thing."

She replied promptly, though her tone was a little distracted. "Just part of a day's work. I get first aid and CPR training every year."

"Kids, huh? How many?"

"No, none."

He was pleased and relieved by her answer. "Nurse?"

"Adult day care. Hold still.... I'm going to probe around the edges of this lump. I can't tell you how sorry I am you got injured."

Adult day care. He thought about that for a while. It didn't jibe, the idea of Abigail as a skilled health care professional and the fact she was a car thief. People who took on that kind of responsibility didn't just walk away from their lives without cause. Nothing about her jibed, not yet.

"Lots of accidents like this in adult day care?"

Her mouth quirked in a rueful smile that made his fingers itch to touch the curling corner and the dimple just beside it. Under the mask of strain she was an attractive woman, if too thin. "If you mean do I take corners too fast when transporting my clients, and give them all head injuries…no. But things get knocked over and break, and then someone tries to help pick up the pieces and gets cut. Or someone will have a seizure. Sometimes the stress is too much for one of them and they think hitting their head on the wall again and again will help. Even obsessively gnawing hangnails until they bleed. Things like that."

Abigail put her palms on his cheeks and tilted his head far to one side. She didn't hesitate to touch his scarred face. *You get points for having balls, Abigail. Most people shy away from that on first sight. Almost none would be willing to touch me.* Her hands were gentle but firm, unintentionally caressing, and an image flitted through his mind of her bending to kiss him. Cade was thankful she couldn't read his inappropriate thoughts. The idea of dragging her ass—and it could be a great ass if she weren't so thin; he'd noticed the upside-down heart shape of it already—to the sheriff in Wildwood appealed less and less.

He was glad he didn't know the deputies in

Wildwood, not the way he knew them here locally in his home jurisdiction of Ocala, or Gainesville, where he'd done undercover work, before the incident that marked him for life. He could just picture himself escorting Abigail into his home station and explaining he'd been stupid enough to leave his truck running and the door standing open like an engraved invitation, and this sweet-faced woman with the capable hands had waltzed off with it.

It would be joke fodder for months. Years. He'd hear about it at every stolen vehicle report, every poker night, fishing trip, birthday parties for their kids, weddings, funerals, K-9 training sessions. The ragging would never end. Even the administrative staff and the dispatchers would get in on the fun.

No. If he took her in, and that was looking like a more remote *if* all the time, it wouldn't be to any station where he was known, either currently or in the past.

She spoke again. "Does it hurt when I press, or are you just stoic?"

"It hurts a little, but I've had worse."

"Really? Hmm." She wetted yet another cotton ball and dabbed some more. "This may leave a scar. I'm sorry about that."

The idea was ludicrous. Compared with the ugly raw meat that was the left side of his face, a half-inch nick in his scalp, easily concealed by hair, was nothing. He tried to hold in his laughter, and ended up shaking silently.

Abigail drew back and stared at Cade. "What's so funny?"

"It might *scar?*" He thrust the left side of his face toward her and said, "Like I said, I've had worse."

She blushed, darkly, and it made her gray eyes sparkle. He couldn't tell whether she was holding back tears or laughter. One knee was up on the bench to balance her, and Cade knew a sudden urge to cup her hips, stroke the long line of her thigh. *What the hell, Latimer? Get a grip, and not on your suspect.*

"Oh. I…see what you mean."

"Yeah."

"Chemical burn? If you don't mind me asking."

"That old standby…acid."

"Did something blow up in your face?"

Yeah...a meth bust went bad. They'd made me and I never knew it. That little twerp and his goon of a buddy... The little twerp was smarter than I thought. I got cocky, and he got lucky, and then I got scarred.

"You could say that." He hoped his tone would discourage more questions, but Abigail just went back to dabbing at the wound as if acid burns were something completely normal.

"It will bleed just a little more, I think. I'm going to put some of this ointment with anesthetic and antibiotics on it. It'll be hard to bandage unless we shave the area."

"No shaving. Does it need stitches?"

"I…don't think so, but I'm going to try a couple of these butterfly bandages on it and see if those help close the gap."

He felt a slight sting as she applied the cream, then it numbed the area of the cut. It was as Abigail was leaning to reach the kit again for the butterfly bandages that her much-washed chambray shirt, minus a button at bra level, gaped open. Where the plackets separated he saw the purple and yellow of bruises, both fresh and fading, on the upper curves of her breasts, where they swelled from the cups of a practical white cotton bra.

Bruises with a definite outline of the too-firm grip of a hand. She hadn't done that to herself.

Cop reflex took over. He gripped her upper arms and brought her upright again where he could review the evidence. She gasped and paled in pain.

"Sit down," he said roughly, rising. He hadn't grabbed her that hard, which only meant she had more bruises elsewhere, as instinct and experience had told him she must. He slackened his grip, but only slightly.

What happened next twisted his gut.

"Please. Please don't. Please. Please. I'll do whatever you want, just please. Don't." The woman was *begging,* scrabbling backward, trying her damnedest to get away, and her voice was filled with the most pathetic dread Cade had ever heard. Cade released her upper arms since it was clear he was causing her pain, and let his hands slip down to her wrists, where he locked his fingers in a grip she would not be able to break easily, even though she had more leverage. She flailed and thrashed, continuing to beg for release, until he caught both wrists in one hand and got close enough to thread the fingers of his free hand into her ponytail and immobilize her. She froze, gazing up with terrified, tear-filled eyes and half-open mouth, breathing as though she'd sprinted a mile.

"Stop. Abigail. Calm down. I don't want anything from you but the truth. That's all."

Her breath came in sobbing, hitching gasps, but she remained still. Holding her gaze, Cade dropped her ponytail and carefully, slowly, turned back the front of her shirt before he looked at the uncovered area he'd glimpsed.

Oh, yes, finger bruises. Someone liked to squeeze her small, pretty breasts to the point of pain and beyond. He bet himself he'd find matching bruises in rings around her upper arms, too. God knew where else. Anywhere they could be easily hidden, no doubt. He knew how abusers worked. Their private, sadistic indulgences were just that, and there would be hell to pay when their victims couldn't conceal the evidence any longer.

Or in Abigail's case, *wouldn't.* This was why she'd stolen his truck. She was running, running like hell.

She bent her head and her ponytail slithered forward over her chest, shielding herself from his gaze.

"Let me see, Abigail. I won't hurt you, but I need to know bruises are the worst of it."

"That…that *crummy* button!" The words came out in the most embarrassed, horrified tone Cade had ever heard a woman use.

He couldn't tell whether the trembling that shook her entire body was laughter, tears, fear, pain or all of the above. She swayed on her feet like an exhausted toddler, and he realized she might fall if she remained standing. He sank back onto the picnic table bench and drew her down with him. She drooped like a flower with a crushed stem, and it was the most natural thing in the world to put an arm around her. In all his thug-tracking days he'd never comforted a criminal like this. How many of them had wept and gazed at him with pitiful, wet eyes? How easily had he withstood those bids for sympathy and lenience? How many of them ended up in the back of the patrol car on the way to jail, where they belonged?

But how quickly, in just moments, had Abigail McMurray and her gigantic problem become the thing he most needed to fix in the world. He felt her stiffness melting away like snow in the Florida sun, and shortly she was leaning against his chest, her hands creeping up to hang on to his shoulders as if he were the only solid thing left on the planet. He took his gun out of his waistband and set it on the ground out of her reach. No sense in being stupid, even if his gut and his crotch were trying so damned hard to overrule his brain.

Now I have the truth.

He had what he thought he wanted, yes. But knowing what had pushed Abigail to take his truck wasn't enough. Now he wanted the man who had done the damage, wanted him fiercely, with a dark, chill fury that was more vendetta than justice. He shouldn't feel this way—his law enforcement training should have kept him from the brink. He hardly knew Abigail, and the fact she'd stolen his truck didn't make her domestic abuse issues his problem.

But somehow they were.

He felt her tears soaking his shirt, her sobs shaking her body, and stared over her head toward the tea-dark river where something had taken the lure on his fishing line and was merrily dragging his pole down the sandy bank into the water.

Aw, hell. You know it's bad when I choose a sobbing woman over the best reel I own. Goodbye, pole. Hello, trouble.

Chapter 4

That twice-damned button.

It had gotten her into this whole mess, rolling under Cade Latimer's pickup in the convenience store's parking lot. Now its lack had made things worse, revealing all the things she had struggled to keep hidden from this observant, determined, fierce man. In her urge to help right at least part of her wrongdoing by tending his head wound, she had unwittingly exposed herself, not to mention Marsh's crimes.

The shame she had felt in all the months before was nothing compared with the burning furnace of shame she felt now as her weakness was revealed.

Yet, in that scorching shame burned the relief that someone else knew at last. The tears flowed in earnest and she began to tremble.

She struggled not to give in to the comfort Cade Latimer was offering. It wasn't right. It wasn't *done*.... She couldn't just weep on a stranger's shoulder. Especially not a stranger whose truck she had stolen. She sank stiffly onto the bench when he tugged her to sit. She fought against his encircling arm—it was just another trap, another trick, another ploy to get her to tell more than she should. He only wanted the lurid details. He didn't want to have to understand, or judge, or help.

It would give him power over her. She could never permit that again.

"Where's your shadow?" Judy asked.

"Looking for a beer."

"Nice of you to bring him."

"Thanks for inviting me. Us. It's good to get out of the house. I haven't seen my friends enough lately."

She felt rather than heard Marsh approach out of her line of sight. He stood behind her, a companionable hand over her left shoulder, squeezing gently.

"Good to see you smiling," Marsh said.

The reminder of Gary made her smile falter. Marsh squeezed her shoulder again and spoke to

Judy. "Abigail tells me your husband's a mechanic. He any good with imports?"

"Japanese, mostly—but he's right over there with the grill. You could just ask." Judy turned her attention back to Abby. "We should do a girls' night out. What are you doing next week?"

Abby opened her mouth to reply, but Marsh's hand squeezed her shoulder again. "We're working on that wheelchair ramp to the back patio," he said.

"But that won't take every night next week," Judy said, smiling.

Abby smiled back. "We could maybe—"

"Things are tight," Marsh interrupted, and this time Abby realized the pressure of his hand was meant to quiet her, to let Marsh take the lead in the conversation. Startled, she lapsed into silence and was rewarded with a gentle rub over her shoulder blade. "We probably should head out. Seven o'clock comes early."

Abby ducked her head and nodded. She really hadn't meant to let Judy know how things were with Gary gone. Marsh set down his beer and she knew he meant for them to leave now. With her evening suddenly soured, she wanted nothing more than to be at home with the covers pulled over her head and maybe the blessed oblivion of a sleeping pill. She gave Judy a quick, embarrassed hug, nodding when Judy said quietly, "Call me. I miss you."

She had simply given the power into Marsh's hands without a second thought.

Abby fought against the bliss of comfort for another minute, but the softening of Latimer's hold was confusing. If he meant to control her, he'd have taken a firmer grip on her. The reservoir of hurt was simply too deep to stem now that the dam had been breached. It was as if the supply of tears was bottomless, salty and hot. She would never be cried out, even after months of mourning Gary and hours of late-night weeping into pillows to stifle her noise so Marsh wouldn't hear. But these tears weren't for Gary. Instead, she was mourning the loss of herself.

Her fingers clenched in his shirt. One by one her hands crept over his shoulders and caught there as if she were clinging to the side of a building, trying desperately not to fall.

Fifteen months with Marsh hadn't erased every scrap of trust, though they'd taken their toll. Every action she took had to be examined and reexamined, for fear it would trigger an unpleasant reaction from Marsh. Now she drowned in the torrent of tears, and Latimer said nothing. Did nothing, except allow her to thoroughly wet his shirt, and keep warm palms cupped at her back. She could feel their heat even past the humid sweatiness of her skin in the heat of the late afternoon. No matter how she gave in to her sobs, some part of her kept guard, alert to any hint of tension in Latimer's body, the telegraphy of imminent violence.

Long minutes later, head throbbing, nose thoroughly stuffed, eyes burning, Abby pulled a scrap of pride from somewhere deep and used it to push back from Latimer. She scrubbed at her face with the sleeves of her shirt, snuffling hard. He made a single quick move and scooped something from the ground as he left the bench—his gun.

When he walked to his truck, Abby sat staring at him. He'd gone from holding a gun on her to turning his back. He no longer considered her a threat. *Of course not, why would he? He's the one with a dog and a gun and the keys.* Her stomach lurched. What would he do with her now? Would his new knowledge change anything? She was still a car thief, no matter how she looked at it.

He came back with a roll of paper towels and put them in front of her. She tore one from the roll and blew her nose. "Thank you." Her voice was thick. Tears were still too near. She knew if she thought even a little about what had happened she would dissolve again.

Latimer set a bottle of water in front of her. "You'll be thirsty after all that bawling."

Abby's glance flicked upward.

He was *smiling.*

She searched his face for mockery, cruelty, for the blankness she had come to associate with

Marsh's concealment of anger, and found none. Instead, there was amusement, and a wry kindness she hadn't expected to see. "You're laughing at me."

"No." He made a short gesture and the dog came to sit at his left. "I don't laugh at women running from domestic violence. Though I have to admit I've never seen it taken to the extreme of stealing a vehicle."

"I'm not—" Abby began the habitual denial, the all-too-familiar lie, and caught herself. Or, rather, was caught by the incisive blue of Latimer's eyes. She looked away, guiltily, and then looked back. *Why am I lying? I never used to lie. I never had a need to lie.* It was part of the way Marsh had broken her, changed her, made her over to fit him.

It was what she hated most about herself, even more than the cowardice that made her second-guess every single word or gesture made where Marsh could hear or see. Even more than the way she cringed away from his physicality. More than the way he controlled every aspect of their lives together. She was relieved her parents were dead and she had no siblings to see what she'd become since Gary's death. She was a nonperson, existing only within the context of Marsh's rigid parameters for approval and acceptance. In her grief, she had distanced herself even from her friends, and they had respected her wishes, letting her be. Her solitude was the perfect environment for Marsh.

"You can't tell me you walked into a door in the middle of the night. Doors don't leave finger marks on your breasts."

Abby looked toward the river, dimpled and purling, glinting in the sun's glare, eddies that spun downstream and faded, the expanding rings of a fish gulping an insect from the surface. She covered her mouth with her hand, drawing a shaky breath through her stuffy nose. Latimer didn't stop her when she got to her feet and moved into the shade of the cypresses at the river's edge.

It was cooler there, with a moistness more pleasant than the sticky humidity of her own sweat in the sunny clearing of the campsite. Her head pounded with the heat and her tear-stuffed sinuses. The breath of the river moved over her skin, luring her closer. She toed off her sneakers and edged her sockless feet into the wet, buff-colored sand at its edge. A foot or two from the shore, she saw a fishing pole beneath the water, its tip bent and caught by a cypress root a few feet out. It must be Latimer's—she didn't see his near the camp stool, and he hadn't brought it back to the picnic table. Abby moved forward two steps, the water rising to her ankles and wetting the slim legs of her jeans.

It felt like heaven, cool and soft and better than iced tea on a hot day. She thought about wading even deeper, diving in and submerging her whole, overheated, exhausted body. She would let the current take her slowly downstream. The tannic water would wash away the salt of tears and sweat, leaching the heat from her shame. She could float wherever the river took her, for miles and days, through the chain of lakes, maybe even on to the Gulf of Mexico. Instead, she rolled up the cuff of her sleeve and plunged her arm into the water to grasp the butt of the rod.

She drew the rod from the water, immediately finding resistance at the far end, where the line had been snarled among the stumps and knees of cypresses and ti-ti shrubs, so she pressed the button on the reel to release the tension, and backed out of the water.

Latimer, who had joined her on the shore, stood at the edge of the water and received the pole from her with a rueful smile. He used his pocketknife to clip the nylon line.

"Sorry, again," Abby said lamely.

"Stuff happens." Latimer shrugged and tilted the rod to empty the water from the reel's spool. "But bruises like yours—that's not the sort of stuff that should happen."

Tears welled and Abby jutted her chin out to stem the flow. "I really, really don't want to talk about it." She picked up her shoes, letting them dangle from two fingers hooked beneath their tongues. No sense trying to jam wet, sandy feet into them.

"I get that, believe me." Latimer followed her to the picnic table, where Abby opened the bottle of water and drank half of it. He closed the blade of the pocketknife and opened another, a screwdriver tip, and began removing the reel from the pole. "But I'm not letting go of the topic for long." His blue gaze flicked up and trapped her. "You can have a break while you build a fire in that grill over there. I want a steak for dinner, since I'm not going to get a chance at a bass or bluegill." His chin jerked toward the truck, where Mort the shepherd lay panting in the shade of the tailgate. "Sack of charcoal back there. Matches in the toolbox."

Abby stared at him, watching as a bead of sweat trickled slowly from his hairline to lose itself in the red, raised maze of his scar. He was disassembling the reel, using paper towels to dry its mechanisms. His hands were quick and deft, with long fingers. They were strong fingers, and gold hairs glittered at the knuckles and along the outer edge of his hands. She set what little she knew about him against the idea of those fingers curling into fists, and found she could not visualize Latimer doing something brutal out of sheer perversity. Unbidden, an image of Marsh's fists came to mind, his strong, stocky fingers and muddy hazel eyes always ready to teach her a lesson.

When she hadn't moved, Latimer looked up at her. "Abigail."

Jolted from her thoughts, she blinked rapidly, scrambling to respond. "What about your dog?"

"He won't bother you unless I give the word. Or you make a sudden move. So don't try something stupid like running away, and you won't have any trouble."

Abby moved slowly toward the truck. Mort was all attention, ears pricked forward, dark eyes unblinking, head turning as she moved. She kept her eyes on him, even as she stretched to reach the bag of charcoal and drag it out onto the tailgate. The matches were a different issue, however, since the toolbox was all the way to the front of the truck bed. She would have to climb in to get them.

She looked over her shoulder at Latimer, who stood at the picnic table with the reel in his hands, grinning. The small jerk of his head indicated she might as well get on with it, so she crept into the truck bed and opened the toolbox.

"That wasn't so bad, was it?" he asked, when she walked past him, still barefoot on the campsite sand.

Abby said nothing, shaking the charcoal into the cement fire ring, slipping a few twigs and dried, crackling live-oak leaves into the pile to catch the flame of the match and hold it long enough to light the briquettes. When a couple of the black squares began to glow at their edges, she got to her feet and went stolidly back to the table. At least the sun was getting low enough to put the table in the shadow of the scrub oaks.

Before an hour had passed, Latimer was cooking a steak on the iron mesh grill of the fire ring, using a fork and his pocketknife to turn and trim the meat. Mort received the tossed trimmings, catching them deftly and snuffling for more. Latimer gave Abby tomatoes to slice on a paper plate, and handed her a can opener and a can of green beans to heat on the grill. When she had finished slicing, he pointedly held his hand out for the return of the steak knife she'd been using.

She wondered if he planned to let her join him in the meal. She shook her head at herself. *Don't be stupid. This isn't a date, Abigail. It's house arrest.* Perhaps he wouldn't make her feel guilty if she fetched her sack of groceries, and opened the chips and chili. Now that she was calmer after the storm of tears, she was hungry. She sat on the picnic bench with the bottle of water, desultorily shooing flies and the occasional wasp from the tomatoes, watching Latimer grilling meat. The label on the green beans slowly charred and flaked away, and steam rose from the can's open mouth. He pushed the can to a cooler spot on the grill.

With Latimer, minding the grill was almost an art form, a choreographed dance. He half squatted, his haunches firm in their blue jeans. She could see the strength in his legs when he rose or crab-walked to stay out of the smoke. In the dance of the grill, there was the bend, the prod of the meat with a fork, the quick flip, the test of the thick part of the steak with the tip of a hunting knife he'd pulled from somewhere on his person. Abby had never even known it was there. Knives, gun. Attack-trained dog. Fishing pole. Camping gear. If she didn't know better, she'd have said Latimer was running away from something himself. The irony made her lips quirk.

He caught the faint smile on her face as he looked up from his squatting position, his leanly muscled body folded in on itself, ready for action. "Smells good, doesn't it?"

"Yeah."

"Get three plates ready. I'm feeling generous."

Abby obeyed without comment, taking paper plates and disposable cutlery from a plastic bin in the back of the truck. She had a couple of bottles of water in her hand when Latimer spoke up.

"Bring me a beer, too, please."

Abby swallowed down her suddenly queasy stomach. Did *everything* have to conjure up Marsh? She visualized her brother-in-law sullenly cracking a can of beer, but in the cooler were only green bottles of lager, and she felt her clenching muscles relax, stupidly relieved to discover it wasn't Marsh's preferred brew. And Latimer had said *please,* a word that had vanished early from Marsh's vocabulary once he had her firmly in his grasp.

"Split the tomatoes and green beans three ways, Abigail."

"Three?"

"You don't think I'm the kind of man who'd deprive my buddy there of this fine meal, do you?" His head tilt indicated Mort, still quiet, tongue lolling, under the tailgate. Abby didn't think the shepherd had taken his eyes off her for the past hour, and was not fooled, despite the doggy smile on his face. "Get a plate over here." Latimer had the fork and knife ready, and lifted the slab of meat onto the plate she held out, with two hands under it to support the weight of the hefty T-bone. He rose, followed her to the table and deftly excised the bone and the fatty edge from the steak, putting them on a second plate with a bit of tomato and green beans. She watched his hands while he carved the meat into two generous portions. There was grace in his handling of the hunting knife.

"I…uh, if you don't mind, I'd like to get the orange juice, and the potato chips, out of…" She looked back toward the pickup.

His eyes shuttered briefly, and Abby saw his calculations, no doubt running through what was in the front seat, potential weapons, perhaps. Then he nodded. She walked to the cab, still keeping an eye on the dog, and reached inside for the juice and chips, bringing them back to the table. As she returned, Mort rose from his place beneath the truck and paced alongside her. Her heart thumped, but the dog merely went to the end of the table nearest to Latimer and sat down again, alert and waiting.

"Sit, Abigail. Eat."

"It's… Abby. Abigail…" She trailed off, settling with the juice and pulling open the bag of chips, pushing them to the center of the table where they might be shared.

"Kinda makes you feel like you might be in some trouble, eh?" His eyes held more than a glint of humor.

"Yeah," she agreed, looking down at the meat on her plate. It was huge, but she was starving, and it smelled delicious. They sat across from each other, Abby and the man whose truck she had stolen, and shared a meal in the slow, blue twilight.

The mosquitoes came out at dusk, just as Cade finished his last bites of steak and beans and chased them with a couple of potato chips and a swig of beer. Mort lay at his feet, working with diligent relish at the T-bone between his paws. Abby hadn't managed all her steak, but she pushed the plate away from herself, one slim hand lying on her belly, and a slightly sleepy look on her face. It was the most relaxed he'd seen her.

Now was the time to get the rest of her story out of her.

"You gonna eat that?" Cade asked, indicating the remaining steak on her plate.

"It was delicious, but I couldn't possibly. Thank you so much. I know I don't deserve your courtesy."

Cade spoke over her. He didn't want to hear her voice turn soft and anxiously pleading now that their casual meal was over. He wasn't her abuser; he didn't want to hear her talking to him as if he were. He'd enjoyed the small talk about camp cooking and the best wood for smoking meat, and whether or not barbecue sauce counted as a food group. "There's this guy I knew, back when I was working a joint task force—drugs—in Ocala." For a moment, he remembered those months, working with the DEA and the local police forces in Ocala. It was his success with the task force that had put him in the limelight and shifted him to undercover work in Gainesville, still with the task force. Undercover work brought a fresh thrill to a job that had begun to seem, if not mundane, at least less of a challenge. Finding and chasing down drug dealers was a matter of patience, diligence and documentation of proof. Undercover work added the spice of risk, the possibility of being discovered and the danger that would bring. The fish were much, much bigger. His sense of fulfillment in a job well done had increased with each successful penetration of an illicit organization.

But then he'd been scarred, and the task force leaders said, "Sorry. No place for a man with a face like that. Wish it had turned out differently." Just like that, his life was over. Understanding the task force's reasons, even agreeing with them, didn't change the way he felt. It was as if he'd wrecked his car into a ditch and would never drive it again.

Once Cade was out of the hospital and back on desk duty, the Marion County Sheriff's Department had offered him an option: take K-9 training to replace a retiring deputy.

Cade jumped. Anything was better than the desk and going home at night to a six-pack of beer and the television.

Working with Mort was more than the consolation prize it had seemed at first. He loved the dog. They made a great team, and Cade didn't have to spend his days with a partner disinclined to work with a man who looked like something out of a Dick Tracy cartoon strip. Cade's work was fulfilling in a different way, but the corner of his soul that craved something more went unsatisfied. He no longer felt as if he was creating, solving, building. He was just taking out the trash, day after day, with a happy four-legged partner.

Mort's zest for every task made the critical difference for Cade, enabling him to stay with a job he—mostly—still loved.

Abby's gray eyes, darkening with the approach of night, flicked to his and pulled him out of the mire of his thoughts. Her thin face drew tight. He could almost hear the click in her brain as she registered *cop,* followed by her immediate return to wariness. He drew the plate toward him, using his hunting knife to cut the strip into four large bites, which he fed to Mort one by one while she watched.

Cade saw her throat move as she swallowed. The air wasn't cooling down with the approach of night. It was still disgustingly humid, but at least the last low rays of the sun lacked their former scorching glare.

"You started to tell me something, Mr. Latimer," she said softly.

"Might as well call me Cade."

There was a long pause, then, "Okay, Cade." As good, as obedient a woman as a man could wish for, even though he plainly heard the undercurrent of renewed suspicion and fear in her voice. His stomach tightened a little. Someone had done a thorough job on her, and he was going to find out why—and who—if it took all night.

"His name was Roy Lewis."

She flinched, but it wasn't at the name. It was

at the mosquito that had found the tender cord of her neck. Her slapping hand left a smear of blood, but her lips flexed in satisfaction at having killed the biting insect.

"Come on around this side. The smoke will keep them away." Cade rose to put their plates on the low-burning coals and added a stick or two of broken scrub oak wood, as well as some fallen brown magnolia leaves. The leaves gave an acrid stink to the smoke. Abby coughed, but moved to his side of the table, sitting to face him on the bench. Her feet were still bare, and she drew them up in front of her, wrapping her arms around her knees.

"So, Roy," Cade continued, settling on the bench again, leaning his back against the table, "he wasn't a bad guy—in fact, he was kinda funny, in that big-dumb-ox way. He got in with the wrong crowd, though. It happens."

She just watched him, listening with her chin on her knees, her hands clenched tight on the arms ringing her legs. She looked prettier by firelight, without the glare of the sun to point out the lines of tension in her face and body. Her thick lashes masked her eyes, but she never took her gaze from him. Cade felt a trace of the old excitement, the frisson playing a role brought. He could make this work.

"We'd been working on this bust for a couple of

months. That night, we made our move. And good ol' Roy, wrong place, wrong time. He thought he was picking up his brother-in-law at work because the man's car had broken down, and instead he was picking up a couple keys of coke along with his brother-in-law. Picked up a tail from the Ocala police and the DEA, too." Cade put a few more sticks on the fire, lighting her thin, pretty face in the gathering dark. The glow highlighted her straight nose and ordinary but eminently kissable mouth. She cleared her throat as smoke puffed past her, but at least the problem of the mosquitoes was temporarily solved.

Cade wet his throat with another swig of beer. "We got to chasing those boys, and eventually Roy wised up and pulled over. But his brother-in-law ditched, sprinted away like a track star, leaving those two keys in the car where Roy was waiting. My partner went after the runner, and Roy and me had us a good long talk." Cade remembered the last time he'd seen Roy Lewis, edging free from that bust because Roy'd sworn on his life and his mother's and everyone else's he knew that he was turning things around. Technically Cade had enough to take Roy to jail, but he'd known the man was trying to get clean and maybe needed just one break, and Cade had given it to him…with a string or two.

Cade let the silence stretch. He looked away,

watching the fire. Eventually Abby bit, as most suspects did, unable to tolerate the silence. "What did you talk about?"

"We talked about those two keys of coke in his car. And his pregnant girlfriend at home. How his record was pretty much clean except for some crap he'd done when he was a few years younger and a whole lot more stupid."

More silence, and Cade knew Abby was wondering what Cade had done about the drugs. Was he a dirty cop? What would she, Abby, do with this knowledge?

In the end, she whispered pitifully, "I don't have anything except a little cash."

Cade had her where he wanted her, though it roiled his guts to have manipulated her so blatantly. "You've got a story, just like Roy had a story. That's what I want, Abby."

She turned slowly to look away from him to the campfire. She waved a little smoke out of her face. Her brows drew together above the bridge of her nose. "You…want me to tell you why I stole your truck."

"Yep." He finished off the beer and walked to the truck for a second bottle. "You want a beer?"

"No, thank you."

"Might make it easier."

"Can I ask you a question?"

"Sure."

"What happened to Roy?"

"What do you think happened to Roy?" He walked back slowly, twisting the cap of the beer off. He tilted the bottle toward her as he sat down, but she shook her head, chin still on her knees.

"That amount of drugs in his car…it's hard to believe he could be lucky enough to walk away."

"Tell me your story, Abigail, and if I like it, I'll tell you what happened to Roy." He knew he was practically giving away the farm, but if she was as smart as he thought she was, she'd figure it out and take the bait anyway. "Why don't you start with his name, get that out of the way."

Her mouth loosened, shook, as her lashes fluttered and firelight flickered on the fresh tears he saw there. Cade stretched out his legs, propping one boot on the edge of the fire ring, and sipped slowly at the beer. Condensation beaded the bottle's sides and softened the paper label. He'd need to buy more ice somewhere tomorrow, top off the cooler again. Pick up more fresh stuff, another steak. Find a place to buy a shower, maybe do a little laundry. Truck stop? Hotel for a night?

There was tonight to get through, too. He didn't yet know how it might play out. Abby didn't show signs of trying to talk him into anything particular, not yet. For now he would settle for prying the details out of her, give him the information he needed to plan, to make a decision between, say, jail or the bus station in Ocala or Gainesville.

It was a good five minutes before she said, "Marsh." She cleared her throat and stopped.

Cade could hear her swallow, and see the flick of her fingers at her eyes, banishing tears. She wasn't even going to try the typical female felon's trick of crying for sympathy while telling her story? Good for her. The action pointed to an unbowed core of strength and self-respect he wanted to encourage.

"His name is Marsh. He's Gary's brother."

Cade hid his grim smile behind the mouth of the beer bottle and his fist at its neck. *Marsh McMurray. Marshall, probably. A man with a name like that can be found.* It would be easy. A telephone call to the sheriff's department in Abby's county, a little courtesy to Deputy Latimer from Marion County, and Marshall McMurray would have a whole passel of trouble in his lap.

Cade thought for a moment about the sequence of events that had led to this moment. If he were still working undercover, he probably wouldn't be on vacation this particular week, depending on what was going on with whatever case he was working. He wouldn't have been at the quickie mart in Wildwood. He and Abby would never have crossed paths. He'd never have met her or felt the impulse to insert himself into her life. Fate, and its convoluted workings, was a hell of a thing.

Marsh moved the Honda twice during the three hours he sat on Drew and Judy's street watching their house. He didn't want to attract too much attention. Each time he moved the car, he drove around the nearby streets for a few minutes before returning and parking in a different spot.

Drew came outside only once, to move a sprinkler to a new place on the thick lawn, and observe its pattern of spray for a few minutes. Judy stood on the front steps, leaning against the door frame with her arms folded beneath her breasts, and watched him. A yappy little dog panted at her bare feet.

There was no sign of Abigail. No curtain twitched at a window, a light didn't go on or off while Drew and Judy were outside.

At 10:00 p.m. the lights went out in the house. Early to bed, early to rise.

Marsh cursed softly, started the Honda and drove into the darkness of Wildwood. Street after street, lights were going out as the sidewalks rolled up in this dinky town. Abigail wasn't on any of them. She wasn't sitting on a bench in the town's sole park. He again passed the convenience store, where the same blonde clerk would close by eleven—nothing in Wildwood stayed open all night except the roadhouse by the interstate. He drove slowly a few streets over, into the business district, and parked far out in the grocery store lot, where he could watch the doors unobserved as the workers inside worked the closing, in case Abigail was waiting there.

It was worrying, not knowing where she was.

Marsh thought about going home to check the answering machine. Maybe she had called. When the lights in the grocery began to flick off bank by bank, he pulled out into the street again.

The house looked no different from when he'd left hours ago, clay still ground into the carpet, empty popcorn bags half spilling from the kitchen trash can, the living room in disarray. Marsh checked every room, but he'd known the moment he opened the door that Abigail wasn't there. The house had a different feel when she was in it. His radar always seemed to know where she was, what she was doing, and he was discomfited now by her utter absence.

Marsh went to her bedroom door and opened it slowly. Her fragrance, light and fresh—something like clean cotton, the scent of baby shampoo and a citrus undertone—lingered in the room like a ghost. The bed was made, the corners of the bed-clothes sharp and crisp, the edges hanging even. He liked that Abigail was tidy.

He flicked on the light and there was Gary,

grinning at him from the wood-framed photograph on the dresser. He remembered that photo from the funeral, where it had stood on a table at the front of the room near the casket, a single spray of bloodred gladiolus in the vase next to the frame. Gary looked mockingly happy in the photo—or maybe it had been Marsh's own tainted happiness reflected back at him. Marsh wasn't happy his brother was dead, but it meant the field to Abigail was clear, and it had given Marsh the easy way inside her guard. If Gary had simply not been Abigail's choice… Marsh fought down the regret. It didn't matter now. It wasn't something he could fix.

But still, everything roiled inside Marsh. Too many emotions fought for supremacy. Anger. Jealousy. Anxiety. Desperation. Love. Fear. Worry. Fury.

He lunged forward and knocked Gary onto his face on Abigail's dresser, satisfied by the ominous crack from the glass. He didn't want his brother smiling at him as he began yanking open drawers and cabinets, looking for a clue to where she might have gone.

At midnight he sat next to the telephone, where the answering machine was as dark as his spirit. His stomach was hot with acid. He knew he should have something to eat, even as late as it was, but Abigail wasn't here to cook, and he was sick of dealing with the kitchen and the clients. He'd found nothing of use in Abigail's room, just box after box of mementos, Gary everywhere. A wedding album. Vacation pictures. Letters, cards. There was even a small bundle of cards Marsh had sent Abigail in the first weeks after Gary's death, cheery greetings, short notes, all filled with the helpful brotherly sentiments of a man supporting his sister-in-law through her grief.

Even now, after the months Marsh had been living with her and begun to mold her to his ways, he was sure Abigail had no true understanding of the depth of his passion for her.

He had loved her before she married Gary, but he'd driven back his need with a ruthless will once she'd made her choice and said her vows to his brother. But fate had given Marsh a second chance, and he wasn't going to let her—his very *life*—slip out of his hands again. She was his.

It was just that simple.

He would do what it took to keep her. She'd learn, given time, where she belonged. Together they would erase the past, erase Gary, and Marsh would fill that space. He could hardly wait for the night when she would come to him, penitent and bare, and he would punish her only a little for delaying his ultimate possession of her for so many months. Punishment would make her utter surrender delicious. Marsh liked the taste of Abigail's tears.

He couldn't think of anyplace else to look for her. He sat, fists clenched, staring straight ahead.

At last he picked up the telephone and dialed.

"Central Sumter Regional Hospital," said a woman who answered on the first ring.

"Yeah…hi, I'm…uh, not sure who I need to speak to, but my…my wife is missing, and it's late and I'm really concerned that…" *My wife.* It would happen. She was that in all but name already, wasn't she? Even if he'd not yet slept with her in the biblical sense, they shared a house, a life, physical intimacy of a sort. He scowled a little. It would help if there weren't so many pictures of Gary around, looking down at him from the walls. Maybe he should take Abigail away—maybe a hotel, without Gary's eyes watching every move he made, would help him consummate their relationship at last. Show Abigail what she did to him, how much he wanted her. Loved her. *Needed* her.

"What's your wife's name?"

"Abigail. Abigail McMurray. She's got long brown hair, gray eyes. She should've been home hours ago."

"Hold on, sir, while I transfer you to the proper department. Someone will help you. Try not to worry."

There was a silence of perhaps thirty seconds.

His heart thumped hard in his chest. Was she there? Had something happened to her, or was the sneaky bitch there to report him for the bruises, the ones he gave her for not holding still enough while he finished taking what pleasure he could—the pleasure she owed him—at her breasts.

"Sir?" It was a different voice, another woman. "Mr. McMurray?"

"Yes?" He tried to keep the pathetic eagerness out of his voice.

"We show no one by that name has been admitted to Regional today."

The knot in his gut eased. "Thank you. Thank you very much."

"You're wel—"

Marsh hung up on her. He didn't need her now, and he didn't have the patience for stupid courtesies.

He needed a drink. Something to help him think more clearly, unwind the tension in his strong, stocky body.

Marsh went to the kitchen and used a key to open the cupboard where they kept the liquor. Everything had to be locked away, or the clients would get hold of it, ruin it, cause trouble. When he had Abigail back, it would be more than time to make a change. Get the hell out of this crappy little town. Jacksonville had so much more to offer the two of them. He could start off at his old job again—he was sure he'd be welcomed back—and Abigail could keep house.

The bottle of rye was lower by more than a couple of fingers when he put his glass down on the counter and rasped his palm over his stubbled cheeks and chin. Abigail wasn't with friends. She wasn't at the stores. She wasn't in the hospital.

That only left the cops, didn't it?

Bitch.

Chapter 5

Ten minutes into her story, when Cade tilted the beer bottle toward her again, this time Abby took it, swallowing down the slightly fizzy, hoppy lager in large gulps. The beer was getting warm, and there wasn't enough in the bottle to do more than take the edge off, but in her agitated, hyperaware state she could feel it hitting her bloodstream in just a couple of minutes. She tried not to think of putting her mouth where his had just been—there was something unquestionably intimate in the action, as if she had committed to trusting him. She didn't want to examine her actions or motives too closely just now; everything was too unsettled, and she knew well the danger of making decisions under duress.

"Sounds like things started out just fine, friendly and all. Helpful when you needed it most." Cade got up again and walked to the truck. Her eyes followed him in the gloom, watching his lean figure. The fire lit him from behind, revealing the fit of his jeans—not too loose, but not too tight, straight-leg jeans that moved with him instead of in spite of him. The orange light also brought out the blued steel of his gun, riding in his waistband. She heard him open the cooler, and the clink of bottles. He came slowly back to the table, his gaze meeting hers, and she realized Cade had let Roy Lewis go. Cade was playing her like a violin, and even though she resented him for it, even if she was falling for his cop line, it felt so good—so boil-lancingly, painfully good—to tell it at last.

Cade sat next to her, closer than he had before. He twisted off the caps and handed her one of the beers. He took a couple of long swigs, looking into the fire. "Go on. Marsh was helpful, pleasant. He was Gary's brother, and you needed help with your day care business. But you couldn't keep steady help, even with the agency looking for staff. Why d'you think that was, Abby?"

"We've got to let her go, Abigail. I caught her looking through Rosemary's wallet."

"Oh, no, surely she didn't, Marsh. She's so good with them, so kind and always gentle—"

"Lots of people talk a good line. Janine got in-

side our guard. We're just lucky we found out now, before she did real damage to someone, or to our business reputation. I should have looked into her background more carefully. I'm sorry, Abigail. It won't happen again."

So Janine had gone. Abby fired the woman herself. Marsh gave her the words to say. "We're going to have to let you go, Janine. We wish you all the best, but we're looking for a more experienced caregiver."

A few weeks later, the woman who had taken Janine's place resigned on her own, citing personal reasons.

The third try was not the charm—the assistant they hired didn't come to work after the first week, and Abby had to call her house and leave a message that she would mail the first and only paycheck to the address she had on file.

They'd all been females, hadn't they? Abby wondered for a moment what might have happened had she wanted to hire a male, but Marsh had helped her screen the applicants and she'd been guided by his advice when it came to hiring.

The answer startled her with its inescapable logic, when it came. How had she not seen it months ago? How could she have been so blinded, so distracted, that she wouldn't notice a trend like that in her own business? "Marsh. Marsh must have…

done something. Run them all off. Lied to them, lied to me. I don't know."

"Why do you think he'd do that?" He turned to look at her, and she was surprised to discover she could still see the blue of his eyes, even in the darkness, lit by the dimming glow of the fire. "Tell me that, Abby."

"Because...because he didn't want anyone finding out about him. About *us.*"

"Is there an *us,* Abby?"

She wanted Cade to stop ending every question with her name. It made her squirm like a bug on a pin, it never let her relax. She had no respite from him, not even for a moment. *Is there an* us, *Abby?*

Yes.

But no.

Hell no.

But yes, in a horrible way, there was an *us.* She and Marsh were linked, through his brutality and her own fear and inaction. Two deformed halves of a twisted, terrible whole. He had broken her to fit him, and she had done nothing to stop him. The shame rose afresh.

"Shut up," she whispered. "Shut up, shut up, shut up!" The words rose to a shriek at the end. "Just take me to jail. That's what you want. Take me to jail for stealing your truck. Get it over with! Go ahead and arrest me, because I'm done telling